What If We Woke Up?

Emma Claire Gannon

Emma Claire Gannon

"I think it's necessary to speak out and stand up for what you believe in, even if you are scared of the consequences. Sometimes, the topics that you're bringing into the light are more important than your pride, ego, or fear of judgment...when you reach a boiling point and become extremely frustrated with the world you have no choice but to live in, you can no longer hold your tongue." (161)

Emma Claire Gannon

What If We Woke Up?

May the snakes of your life
  Be ever garden variety

Emma Claire Gannon

Contents

1. The Guidance Counselor
2. The Mother
3. The Beginning
4. The Writer
5. The Gay Man
6. The Runner
7. The Immigrant
8. The Woman
9. The Teenager
10. The Homeless Man
11. The Hippie
12. The Bartender
13. The End

Emma Claire Gannon

The Guidance Counselor

The office of a Massachusetts high school guidance counselor was bright and cheery on one of the first nice days of spring. The snow was beginning to melt, and for the school administrators, the change in the season meant another class was only a few weeks away from their graduation. It was the guidance counselor's job to interview the seniors for the yearbook, and Monica Lewis was next on the list.

"Is that what I should want? Should I throw my life away because that's what everyone else does? Who said that I needed to conform? Who decided that you should even ask me that question? You know how you should word it? Do you want to live, or do you want to watch your life fly past you, never stopping to think about what you really want?

"How many people can honestly say they're happy? How many people can say they're satisfied? My bet is not that many...not that many at all. Is it because they've never been given the opportunity to figure out who they are? It seems to me most people never really live. They just follow whatever everyone else is doing. They blindly obey their teachers. The teacher doesn't walk out of your life as you age; they just morph into something else. The petite, young woman that teaches first grade becomes the grumpy old man that teaches high school and then the college professor, who doesn't know how to format a presentation, and then the boss, who thinks of you as nothing more than another robot he has to program and occasionally retune. Then what happens? Is it the medical student trying to get hours in at the local hospice? The funeral director? Is that when whatever you believe the afterlife is begins? Is this when you get to meet whatever gods you believe in?

"Can I be honest? I've waited eighteen years for my life to start, and now, sitting in front of you, I know it's getting closer every single day. I'm almost done waiting. Sure, people are going to ask me why I'm throwing it all away. I've always been told that I'd make a good pediatrician; at least that's what my grandmother thinks. I think I'd be better at law; that's what my mother thinks too. I don't know, though. As interesting as that sounds, it doesn't make me want to spend the rest of my days answering 'what do you do?' with what everyone expects of me.

"I don't understand why anyone would willingly give up the chance to live to make a few extra bucks. Why is reproducing our only real purpose in life? Sure, it's necessary, if we want to continue the drudgery, but why is it what we live for; why is that the expectation; how do I know there's not something more?

"I know it might be hard to follow, especially if you've already conformed, as you have, and don't take it personally, but I know that somewhere out there, there's someone that wants to live the same way I do. They just need one more push. Maybe I can help them live. I'd like to be an example. Not one that's remembered in history textbooks, but one that, even if just for a moment, even if they don't know my name, can inspire people to truly live.

"When it rains I want to stand in the middle of the street, collecting the drops, savoring them, swallowing them, making them a part of me, getting to know what the earth really tastes like. When it's windy I want to stand in the middle of an open field in a sundress and let the wind whip me around, not caring if I fall. When the tide is high I want to swim in it. When the tide is low I want to fish in it. If the birds are singing I want to dance along. If a tree is falling I want to be there to make sure someone hears the crash.

"We only get one life, and it's not even a long one, so I'm not gonna let mine continue to pass me by without any of my own input.

"I know it sounds crazy, and people are going to tell me that the logistics are all wrong. You need to find a way to live, a way to survive. That's why I'd like to personally guarantee you that I will find a way to live. I promise you. I don't know what it is yet. I don't know what it looks like. To be honest, I don't know where it is. I don't know who it's with. I just know that I want... no, more than want...I need to live. As long as I do that, I will be satisfied. As long as I don't give in, as long as I don't conform, I won't regret anything.

"I think people are afraid of death only because they haven't lived. If you do what you've set out to do, if you've accomplished your goals, not even all of them, but the strongest, the most important of them, you won't be afraid. That's when you know you've lived. I'd very much like to get to that point, and I have every intention to do so.

"I can't picture myself enjoying the mundane. To be completely honest, I'm not sure how many more years I'd get through before deliberately taking a long walk off a short pier. That's what society wants. Essentially, they want their expectations to drive me to my death. When you put it like that it doesn't sound as practical anymore, does it? I don't think so.

"They want me to wake up never feeling fully refreshed. I look over, and I see some ungrateful man lying next to me. To be completely honest, I don't know who he is. I don't know the first thing about the man I married, the man I promised to protect in sickness and in health. Is he even real? He's probably cheating on me, but I'm not going to say anything. I don't want to have to try to keep myself from crying through another argument. I don't think I wanted to marry him at all, not even in the first place. I didn't know who he was then, and I still don't. Sure, he was nice to me, and he took me out to dinner, and he whispered things in my ears that a prospective husband should say to his future bride, but did he believe any of what he was saying? Did I believe any of what he was saying? Did I convince myself I did for a ring?

"I think it was my mother. I think she's the reason I said yes when he kneeled down in an overpriced, low quality, knock-off restaurant. She liked him. He had a job. What do we want him to be: an accountant? Sure, that sounds about right. He worked for a company with locations across the country. They even had one in Canada. My mother liked that. She liked that it was fairly stable. She liked that we would have the freedom to move around a little bit more than the regular *couple*; he could transfer to another branch.

"Then he got me pregnant. Twice. Back to back. He said if we were gonna do it, we should do it immediately. He was only two years older than his brother, and he thought if they were even closer in age they would have had a stronger bond. That's what he wanted for his children. Wanting to be the perfect wife, I obliged. Sure, do whatever you want with my body; we're married, it doesn't matter.

"Flash forward...what do we want to say: five years? Flash forward five years. They're both in school and daycare now, and they don't really fight yet, but you know it's coming. It gets closer every day. You're terrified of it. You just want the perfect American family: the suburban house, the white picket fence, the minivan, the nine-to-five, the two kids, the dog, and the goldfish. Maybe you can even throw in a senile grandfather if you're so inclined. That's what you've been led to believe, anyway.

"Is that what America is? Is that the modern American dream? In a world that never stops evolving, why are we so stuck on an idea that seems so primitive, so old fashioned in nature? If I wanted to marry a woman, my cat, the three-hundred-year-old pirate ghost that lives in my basement, why can't I do that without being looked down on by others? Why can't I make decisions for myself simply because I want to?

"The same goes for careers. If I wanted to be a neurosurgeon, they'd say 'we're so proud of you.' If I wanted to be a rocket scientist: 'look at you go!' If I wanted to be a writer: 'what's the backup plan? You know that's a hard industry to get into.' That's what everyone tells you. Your math teacher thinks you're too good to be a writer. If you want to be a bartender, a porn star, a grocery bagger suddenly there's an issue. Sure, when people say you'll need some money saved to start a family, they're not lying, but why is anyone assuming me and my pirate husband want kids in the first place? What if my passion in life was making sure eggs got a bag to themselves?

"Why do we as a society feel the need to look down on certain people, maybe simply just because they've had back luck, or they've fallen on hard times, when we display other people up on flashy golden pedestals?

"Some neurosurgeons are waist-deep in paperwork and don't sleep because they're worried they might botch their next surgery. They're drowning in student loans, and they have to go to special, upper-class practices just to make a dent in their debt and therefore can't help the people of the inner city they grew up in. Their spouse is about to leave them because they're not getting enough attention, and the only opinion about the pending separation that their kids have is that they're going to get two Christmases. Now tell me you still think they're smarter than the bartender at the local dive, who has no student debt, can pick up at any time and go wherever the wind takes them, and gets to talk to people: conscious people. Maybe, the bartender and the neurosurgeon will cross paths when the latter's spouse finally leaves them, and they turn to the only coping mechanism they have. I don't know about you, but I'd rather be the one pouring."

Monica Lewis sat opposite the tired-looking woman in her late forties that was supposed to be guiding and counseling Monica's young life. Monica, at eighteen, was only a matter of days away from the destination she had worked at for twelve years: high school graduation. She thought after her name was called, she walked across the stage, almost tripped, and took a piece of paper out of the principal's hand, who would not recall having ever seen Monica in the hallways of her Massachusetts high school, her life would finally begin.

    Monica Lewis would not be remembered by many (if any at all) of her classmates. She never joined any teams, she never participated in any clubs, and she never had any true friends. She had a few acquaintances that she sat with at lunch who stared at their cellphones, sending pictures of themselves clothed to the girl sitting next to them and unclothed to the boy across the cafeteria.

    Monica was too much of a free spirit to be accepted by her more literal classmates. She spent her afternoons walking through the woods behind her house, taking in the trail.

    This was not how her peers lived. After the final bell at the end of the school day, some would take off to work a shift at the local fast-food chain. Some would head to practices to be belittled for not hustling. Some would head straight home and study until they fell asleep with their textbooks in their laps at two o'clock in the morning, their faces stained with anxious tears, and some would head to the railroad tracks between the middle and high school to indulge in more than just a few vices. The police turned a blind eye to this blunt-littered section of town, and the school administration had no legal power to enforce any of the standards listed in the student handbook.

    Monica Lewis found engaging in any of the aforementioned activities nothing but trivial. While her classmates argued over the answer to the previous night's homework, her family members chatted about the weather, and her teachers recapped the previous night's game, Monica Lewis pondered the meaning of life and death. She didn't need a definitive answer as to the purpose of life; in fact, she liked not being guaranteed. She found these philosophical questions more intriguing than the conversations the people around her partook in.

When Monica heard the "wise" characters in books, television shows, and real-life say that people don't talk about anything anymore, she couldn't help but disagree.

She thought that people never really talked at all. Even in her short eighteen years of life, Monica had realized that even though humans are the only known species with a complete and formal language, they are horrible at using it. She firmly believed that the only reason people talk at all is to hear themselves. No one listens; no one ever did. Instead of listening, people just wait to add information about their own lives, every so often coming back to consciousness to make sure what they're about to say still makes sense in context.

This was precisely why she would not be remembered by her classmates, the people her grandmother thought she spent her time dancing and drinking her youth away beside. Monica Lewis never mentioned her eternal loneliness to her grandmother, who was a regular attendee of the bingo nights at the local community center and could not come to grasp the concept of introvertedness.

Monica would never attend a high school reunion. Monica would never be added to a group chat with her classmates. She would not be recognized when her former classmate's future kids asked for a backstory on the girl in the yearbook.

Yet, Monica could not have been more content with her outcast self. She found solace in her thoughts, experiences, and beliefs. Monica did not need someone to reassure her of her own existence. She knew who she was and was not afraid to tell anyone who explicitly asked.

In a world that strives for nothing more than social acceptance, Monica was the outlier. She did not need other people, many of whom struggled to understand themselves, to advise her life. Included in this group was her high school guidance counselor, who sat opposite Monica, mouth hanging open after listening to the girl slight her life choices.

"What do you want me to put?" were the only seven words this astounded woman could utter.

Monica could not remember what the original question was and therefore asked for a reiteration from the guidance counselor. (As much as Monica despised people talking only of themselves, she had just spent the previous ten minutes lecturing the woman on her theories about life. Although she thought her expressions were deeper than the conversations (or really, ping-pong games of one-sided syllables) that other people engaged in, she had, in essence, just done the exact same thing. The opinion one may form of Monica may vary significantly, from conceited, arrogant, and selfish to wishful, understanding, and optimistic. The beauty is in the eye of the beholder.)

The guidance counselor repeated her question. (She was never one to underestimate the effectiveness of an annoyed undertone.)
"What do you plan on majoring in? I need something to put in the yearbook."
Monica Lewis stared back at the woman, debating her response for a moment. She, in fact, did not plan on majoring in anything; she had no plans to further her education whatsoever. She understood the ever-growing importance of educational enlightenment to open professional doors. Essentially, a bachelor's degree was the key; a graduate's degree was the water displacement spray. However, even with this clear understanding of the effects her decisions would have on her very-near and quickly approaching future, Monica did not waver.
"Well, I don't know what you'd put. It seems rather odd that there isn't another option, no?"
"Yeah. You already told me that."
After a moment of uncomfortable silence, Monica asked the woman for permission to ask a question.
"Is this one gonna be a little quicker? I have ten more kids I need to talk to before lunch, and I'm already behind schedule."
Monica was happy to put a limit on her response. (Although she didn't understand some topics of the adult world (she believed most adults don't either. Essentially, aging to Monica simply meant outgrowing old shoes and

becoming too proud to play with cars and dolls), she did understand the value of time. She understood how truly limited it is for each individual.)

"Sure, I can do that." Monica paused briefly, her gaze falling on the wall behind the woman. She did not say anything for a few seconds, and, in that time, the woman took a shallow, annoyed breath.

"You were gonna ask a question?" Monica looked back at the woman, squinted her eyes, and cocked her head to one side.

"I forgot what I was going to say."

The woman shook her head, once again annoyed by the time this girl had wasted. Over the course of Monica's four years under the guidance of this woman, she had spent many an hour in her office. Monica had sometimes even eaten her lunch in the room in an attempt to avoid the teasing that would have accompanied sitting alone in the cafeteria. Other times, teachers were concerned by Monica's apparent lack of social stimulation and called the only form of intervention the school could offer: an underpaid, underprepared, and overtired woman.

This woman had grown increasingly tired of Monica's presence, but to ensure she could afford to put meals on her table for her children, she forced herself to at least pretend to listen.

Oftentimes, this woman would play card games on her computer while Monica vomited another rant about her grievances with life. More often than not, the woman would take offense to Monica's statements, getting the impression that she was being judged for the decision she had made many years prior to follow her dream of aiding the youth of America. There was not a day that went by when she didn't regret that decision.

However, the counselor's favorite pastime while half-listening to these always impassioned spiels was to drown them out completely.

The woman would close her eyes, imagining a turquoise ocean stretching out in front of her sandy feet. This woman would never visit a Caribbean beach in her life, but she thoroughly enjoyed pretending she could. The most ironic part of this controlled-hallucination was she pictured herself lounging in the small bikini she saw while walking into the supermarket to pick up the week's groceries, (she sweat more watching the cashier ring up her milk and bread than she would have on a tropical beach) but she never would have bought it for herself. The image she had of her own body was significantly different than the woman Monica saw.

Monica understood that she was more often than not ignored by this woman and amused herself injecting ridiculous details into her speeches. In four years, Monica's mother had been seven and a half feet tall, she had been the heir to the British throne, and her science teacher had been bribing her to come to his house on Friday evenings. The last part wasn't much of a stretch; Monica herself just hadn't been one of the few that accepted the offer in exchange for extra credit on tests.

The counselor never even heard these details, and if she had, she would have ignored them entirely.

"You forgot?"

Monica, as always, sensed the aggravation in this woman's voice. Monica felt confident even her "I do" was declared in that tone.

"Yeah. Sorry." The woman took a deep breath.

"That's it?"

"I think so." Monica nodded her head, and it finally dawned on the woman that she would never have to guide Monica again. She didn't hate Monica; in fact, it was just the opposite. She had a level of respect for the girl that surprised even herself. Although she did not understand her logic or absolute disgust for the mundane, this woman respected Monica's stubbornness and passion.

She stood up from her chair, hoping the action would send the right message to Monica, who rose in response.

"Well," said the woman. "Good luck." A smile passed over her face, and Monica noted this was the first time she had seen such a sign of affection from the woman.

"Thank you." Monica turned and walked out of this woman's office for the last time, never looking back.

The counselor was surprised that the girl who had so much to say had ended their relationship with two words. She was relieved, however, she would never have to listen to another Monica Lewis tirade.

The Mother

"Are you insane? Are you out of your mind? I'm sorry, what? I raised you better than that. Now you're just going to be an idiot, disgrace your mother, disgrace your family's name? What's wrong with you? I don't remember dropping you on your head as a child, but now I'm not so sure."

Monica's forty-three-year-old mother took a breath for the first time in about half-a-dozen sentences. She was an attractive woman, but with her face red and her tone hysterical, she looked almost unhinged as she stood over her teenage daughter, supporting her weight on the back of the empty chair across from Monica, who was sitting.

Monica's mother, legally named Katherine but referred to as Kate by those who knew her best and as a derogative "mother" by Monica, had been so alluring in her youth that she had attracted the attention of the top salesman at a local used car dealership. This man, who called himself Christopher but Owen while filing his taxes (Christopher did not legally exist), asked Katherine to dinner the day he laid eyes on her.

After a whirlwind year of romantic adventuring, the law finally caught up with the salesman, and Monica's mother never saw her lover again.

Although Monica's father may have overlooked some fine details, which lead to his eventual demise, he had put a significant amount of money into a Swiss bank account, which was supposed to be used to get Monica into the finest high school in Massachusetts. (Monica's mother had invested some of the money in a local nail salon, which turned out to be another front, something Katherine seemed to naturally gravitate towards.)

"You think you can just run around and forget everything I taught you? Jesus, Monica, this is embarrassing. What am I supposed to tell my friends? All of their kids are going to college and getting actual jobs. What am I supposed to say? My loser of a daughter wants to waste her life? 'Oh, I need to be different. Look at me. I'm so unique.'" Monica's mother began laughing maniacally. "'Everything's about me. I can't think of someone other than myself for half a second.'" Katherine's gaze tightened on her daughter, and her laughter ceased. "Give it up. You're not special. You're not remarkable. You're just like everyone else. Get off your high horse and get a grip. You're going to college. You're going to major in something that I can brag about at the hair salon, and that's the end of it. I don't want to hear any more of this nonsense. I don't care what you want. You're going to thank me later. You're welcome."

Monica stared back at her raving mother, a blank smile over her face. Monica could have very well listened to a lullaby based on her expression.

"Are you done?" This only infuriated Katherine even more.

"The disrespect. God, I'm doing this for you. You're too stupid to realize that I'm doing you a favor? You can't even thank me? I had one chance. Your father had one chance, and you're going to blow it for both of us so you become a hippie? It's disgusting. It's appalling. It's revolting."

"Have you been studying a thesaurus?"

"What?" Katherine eyed her only daughter, her expression becoming even more hysterical. Her eye began twitching, and her breathing grew even more sporadic.

This, however, was nothing new in the Lewis household. There was one blurry polaroid of Christopher taped to the refrigerator, but that was the only influence he had on the only two women of his life (not including his late mother, who had spent her evenings playing bingo and sipping martinis instead of helping her three sons with their algebra homework).

Monica would have preferred if their twelve-hundred square foot Massachusetts house (not home) was simply the Monica Lewis household whereas Katherine would have preferred the Katherine-Kate-Katie-Mother-Ms. Lewis household starring Katherine Lewis in all roles.

Katherine was not a horrible role-model for Monica (she was much better than her own mother had been), but Monica desired a little more freedom and a little less structure than was offered. Although Katherine had often offered a helping hand to guide Monica's life, more often than not those therapy sessions turned into screaming matches that one time even resulted in a noise complaint from the neighbors.

At heart, Katerine was a traditional mother with a tradition-hating daughter. Monica didn't despise her mother and would eventually come to miss the smell of her shampoo and perfume. She did truly appreciate every sacrifice Katherine had made for her and understood, at that moment, sitting across from her wheezing mother, she had simply caught an already annoyed Katherine off-guard. She knew it would only take a few words to diffuse the volatile woman and even fewer to change her opinion.

"I have opened every door for you. I worked a lot harder than I should have just to make sure you could go to a decent school. You're ignorant. You don't understand the position you're putting me in, get it? I have saved money for years, money that could have gone to fixing this place up, going on a vacation, going to a restaurant more than once a year. God, I don't even know what I could have been doing with that money." Katherine slammed her fists against the table, her acrylics clattering against the cloth, which was a hand-me-down from Katherine's younger sister, who had found success in the pyramid scheme that is beauty sales. If Monica's mother had saved money, which she had (in fact, she put away everything she could to ensure her daughter's professional and educational aspirations were feasible), she had also allocated the funds to ensure her fingernails were painted in the newest, brightest colors.

She had to compete with Barbra down the street, of course. Barbra's son had become one of the most sought-after surgeons in the greater Boston area (he had worked his way up the ladder after it was discovered his superior had been hiding a camera in the waiting room's bathroom), and Katherine had promised herself that her daughter would reach an even higher level of professional success by becoming one of the area's most sought after lawyers just to spite Barbra.

"When you were younger, I was proud of you. I was proud that you didn't feel the pressure to follow the crowd, but I thought that was something you were gonna grow out of, just a phase. You're too stubborn to understand that the world isn't just some magical place filled with butterflies and fairies where everyone rides off happily into the sunset. Grow up. It's not cute. You're not eight anymore, so stop acting like it."

Katherine looked away from Monica, taking a moment to compose herself. She always tried to keep her emotions in check, never allowing herself to become the overbearing, all-controlling individual her mother had been.

As confused by Monica's wishes as she was, she did not want her only child to ignore her pleas to come home for Thanksgiving.

"Is it my turn now?" Her question had gotten her mother's attention, and Katherine looked back at Monica, who was entirely unfazed, a smug smile resting on her lips.

"Fine." This tone was far less aggressive than the one the guidance counselor, who had become nothing more to Monica than a fleeting memory, had used on her in all their face-to-face meetings. After confessing to that woman, Monica decided to finally tell her mother about her vision for her future. This, however, was nothing new. She had been leaving clues foreshadowing the announcement of her dream for the better part of two years. She was unsure of how much Katherine had picked up on.

"But you have to promise not to interrupt; I'll tell you when I'm done." The golden rule of the Lewis household denoted that everyone got a fair chance to speak. Both Monica and Katherine believed that open conversation without injection of judgment was the best way to solve a problem.

Because of this golden rule, Katherine answered: "Of course."

Monica patted the table in front of her with her palm, inviting her mother to join her. Katherine pulled out the chair and sat down, staring directly into Monica's eyes.

Monica picked up the glass of water resting in the middle of the table and took a long sip, nearly emptying the glass. Katherine preferred her water with ice and lemon, but Monica drank hers from the tap. Even though people swam and drove their diesel-engined boats through the lake that was the town's water supply, it was famous for being one of the best tasting tap waters in the area. It was also infamous for its high levels of uranium and lead.

"My entire life I've been told what I should do," was the way Monica began her rebuttal. I've been told that I should be a doctor, a lawyer, a teacher, or an engineer, but never once has a single one of those options made me excited for the future. I know I'm being selfish; I do. Believe me, and I know it's putting you in a very awkward position. I don't want to hurt you, and that's why I never explicitly told you any of this before. I guess, in keeping quiet, I was not only protecting myself from judgment and ridicule, but I was also protecting you. This isn't meant to make you out to be the bad guy; it's actually the opposite. You can be disappointed in me if that's what you think the proper response is, but at the end of the day, I'm just trying my best. I'm trying my best to remain true to who I am in a world that aspires to take nothing but your individuality. I do believe dreams are killed by logistics. I really do. I think the education system and the way we look down at certain majors and artists and interests kills more dreams than death itself. I don't have a dream. I don't want to become an artist, I don't want to become famous. I want to live. I want to wake up in the morning and watch the sunrise. I want to watch the sunset at the end of the day. I know how expensive it is just to breathe; that seven-twenty-five an hour isn't gonna get you that far, but I don't *need* to get far. If I do decide that after a while I am ready to accept the norm, that I am ready to conform, I will come back, and I will go to college. I'll get a real job, and I'll give you a son-in-law and a couple of grandkids and granddogs. I just need to do this now, because if I don't, I never will. I'll never be as free as I am right now."

Katherine took a deep breath and looked away from her only child. Her anger had been replaced by an almost indescribable sadness. After a moment, she looked back at Monica and nodded her head affirmatively. Monica took this simple motion as a cue to continue.

"I'm sorry I have to do this to you. I really am. You deserve so much better."

"You don't *have* to do this to me. You could suck it up and pretend to be normal."

"You promised not to interrupt." Unenthusiastically, Katherine agreed. "I promise you, I'm going to be okay, and soon enough we might look back on this and laugh. You're going to tell my children about the crazy idea their mother had when she was younger. I wouldn't want my children to do what I'm doing to you right now, but, personally, this is the only option I find desirable, and I'm not willing to give it up."

Kathrine laughed slightly, but the puff of air read more like one of disgust than joy.

"You're right. I don't get it, but I don't think I have much input. You're young, Monica. You are, and when you look back when you're my age, you're going to realize how foolish you look. As a mother, this is the moment I was terrified of: the moment you realized you could make decisions for yourself, and you didn't need me to hold your hand. The moment you realized we have nothing but free will, and no one can ever make you do something you don't want to do. Now I realize there was no moment of epiphany for you; you've known all along. I am proud of you. I really am. I guess there's nothing I can do to stop you. I don't know what I'll tell my friends (I think they'll think less of me now), but I guess your opinion of me is the only one that really matters." The pair sat in silence for a moment, both looking away from each other. They each knew what would happen next.

"I guess all I can say is good luck."

Monica looked up at her mother and smiled.

"Thank you. I really do appreciate it."

Katherine took a deep breath, expressing her discontent with the situation. However, she knew Monica's opinions would not waver, and there was nothing left to do but agree. This was not the first time Monica had swayed her mother's decisions, but it would be the last. One of the only positions in Katherine's life that Monica had been unable to bend was her unwavering belief that the pair should not adopt a dog. (Katherine's pet dog had run away when she was in elementary school.)

"So you're gonna drive?" Katherine looked back at Monica.

"Yeah. That's the plan anyway." Monica let out a light laugh for the first time in a while. She felt that in telling her mother her goals and aspirations, a weight had been lifted off her shoulders. She no longer carried the world and its expectations around with her.

"Where are you gonna go?" Katherine looked to be almost on the verge of tears.

"I don't know yet; that's the beauty of it. I'm gonna get in the car, and I'm gonna drive. Maybe I'll look at a map, maybe I won't. I don't know where I'll end up. That's why I'm excited."

"You realize that makes me even more nervous: not knowing where you are?"

"I know. I don't want to do that, but I'll call you. I'll update you every day. I'm gonna be all right, I promise."

"I don't like this." Katherine hunched over, collecting her sagging head in her hands. "I really don't." Monica reached out and touched her mother's shoulder. This simple tap had a calming effect on Katherine, one that even she did not understand.

"Unfortunately, this is the position we find ourselves in," said Monica before retreating her hand back to her side of the table.

In the eighteen years of Monica's existence, the kitchen table had become a war zone on multiple occasions. Instead of sharing bites of cake and stories about their family's past, these two women had launched torpedoes and nuclear bombs across the twenty-year-old wood. On this night, the atmosphere was significantly less hostile than it had been on other occasions.

One of the most devastating battles came around the time of Monica's tenth birthday when she requested to have her ears pierced because everyone on the playground was making fun of her for being the only girl whose ears were not bedazzled. (Monica had only ever had acquaintances. When she was younger, she would spend some of her hours at the homes of her friends' parents', snacking and talking about the schoolyard gossip and not much else. This was around the same time Monica concluded that most of the conversations humans have are of little importance. It took her another year or two to realize this phenomenon is not unique to the twenty-first century.

Around the same time as the piercing debate, her acquaintances realized they desired to roll with a more popular crowd and left Monica alone with the leftovers and other outcasts. She would go the rest of her school career bouncing between lunch tables to avoid being labeled as the girl who had no friends.

As strong as her personal opinions were, she would do anything to avoid public humiliation. She never volunteered to answer questions from her teachers in fear that she would get the answer wrong and become the laughing stock of the class. Even teachers, sometimes unintentionally, would join in on the taunting. Did they ever outgrow their own high school habits? Monica thought not.

The most ironic part of Monica's struggle to fit in with the normal crowd was that she would have been a loyal friend. Although she may have been too intimidated by her peers to stand up for herself, she would have taken a hit for a friend of her own.

  The only time Monica had experienced a glimmer of friendship from someone with a high social status was in seventh grade when the captain of the middle school cheerleading team, who, based on the way she talked about her flyers and tumblers, believed that the world revolved around a semi-decent, twenty-member, division-two, middle school girls cheerleading team. The only boy that had intended to try out for the team was turned off by the sexist and heckling nature of the head coach and her eating-disorder-plagued team.

  To participate in the gym class activity that day in seventh grade, Monica and her classmates were instructed to find partners. This caused much additional stress for Monica and her socially-anxious peers. Monica remained seated, looking around, hoping that her facial expression appeared so desperate that someone else would pity her enough to offer their partnership.

  Monica preferred it when teachers assigned partners, even if she ended up with the girl that did not care about her grades because it meant she could end up doing all the work herself (she was more confident in her own ability than others). More often than not, however, she ended up with a social outcast, who was the subject of many a passed note. She feared that by association with such a student, her name would be added to the margins of those notes.

  However, this was not the case that earth-shattering day in gym class. One of the most popular girls in the school, who was the head cheerleader and a straight 'a' student (she cheated on every test and convinced the morally gray teachers to look the other way), had asked Monica to be her partner in a game she would have forgotten the next day had it not been for Brittany's superficial kindness.

    In truth, Brittany's best friend, Theresa, had left school for a doctor's appointment the period prior and Brittany came to the life-altering realization that she only had friends when Theresa was around. Essentially, Brittany was only friends with Theresa, and Theresa was popular. Luckily for Brittany, her parents made enough money annually to get her a therapist.

    This was why she asked Monica to be her partner: to avoid the heckling that would have followed a general consensus surrounding her social status. Monica, sensing there was some foul play at work, was skeptical but didn't want to cause a scene. Monica lost interest, however, when Brittany made a snarky comment about another girl's natural weight gain.

    Monica was entirely aware of her social status in the minefield of public education and often laughed at its foolishness. Monica had more "friends" than Brittany did, but because Brittany was desperate enough to go looking for reassurance from her peers, who were looking for the same themselves, she was higher up on the social ladder. Brittany could braid hair. Brittany could do a cartwheel and talked poorly about her classmates. These were the only prerequisites for popularity.

    Monica kept quiet enough to remain an anonymous member of the middle class. In fact, when her name was eventually called during the long-awaited graduation ceremony, there was a general rustling from her peers in the crowd turning around to ask each other *who is she*?)

When Monica sat down at the kitchen table at age ten requesting that her mother paid for her social acceptance by driving to the mall and getting two holes punched in her body, Katherine was entirely indifferent to the situation (she had had her ears pierced around the same time in her own life). She was happy to help her daughter avoid the neighborhood bully, who was four feet tall and wore pigtails but was menacing nevertheless. However, after working a ten-hour shift, she wanted nothing more than to put her feet up and watch her favorite rom-com for the thousandth time without interruption.

Monica generally gave her mother the personal space she needed, and Katherine tried to do the same for her rapidly developing daughter. However, at ten years old, Monica was not yet strong enough to ignore the taunting from her peers and demanded that they make the trip across town immediately.

The shouting match that ensued was the loudest and most intense in Lewis family history.

The one that transpired as a result of Monica's desire to evade the mundane was not nearly as impassioned. Katherine, eighteen years overdue for a long-awaited nap, could do nothing but give in to her daughter's wishes.

Monica knew she had won.

After a long moment of cognitively taking the necessary steps to avoid a new argument-intensity record, Katherine finally responded: "You know it's my job to worry about you."

"Sure," Monica replied in a tone suggesting she was aware of this fact.

"And it makes me even more nervous that I won't know where you are at all times."

"I understand that. Here's my defense-"

"I told you should have been a lawyer."

"I still can be; maybe I will. I just don't know yet, but don't give up on me. I'll give you something to tell Barbra about."

"Did you hear her son got promoted?"

"Yeah, only cause they had to fire the other guy."

"What a pervert." Katherine's body shuddered.

Monica's eyes softened, signaling she was about to present her counterargument.

"You've watched me for eighteen years."

"Very closely."

"And I think I've done a decent job proving to you that you can trust me." Katherine understood that Monica was attempting to make it harder for her to deny her of her wishes and was succeeding. "I haven't succumbed to any of the typical teenager things that parents are so scared of. I took one sip of rum one night when you left it on the counter, but I immediately spit it out in the sink." Katherine let out a slight laugh. "I think I deserve to be trusted. Maybe I don't understand how the world works. Maybe I don't understand what it's like in places that aren't here, at this table, but I promise you that I will adapt. I will learn. I know this isn't what you pictured for me, but I think the fact that I'm close enough to you to tell you how I actually feel and I'm not so afraid of your judgment that I'll do anything to please you goes to prove that you have done everything you could have. That's why I truly am sorry."

Katherine smiled lightly in response.

"Sometimes I think you're a lot older than you are."

"Really?"

Katherine nodded affirmatively. "And other times I think you're a lot younger than you are."

Monica smiled and let out a soft laugh. "Sorry I'm inconsistent."

Monica and Katherine shared one more laugh. They were rapidly bleeding their limited store of shared laughter. They only had so many giggles left between the two of them.

"It's all right. I don't think I was so consistent myself when I was your age. I'm not so sure I'm consistent now."

"This isn't the end, mother; it's not. You'll see me when I come back. I'll call you every night." Katherine smiled back, a noticeable pain in her eyes.

"I got really lucky," was Monica's way of ending the conversation. "I couldn't have asked for a better, stronger role-model."

"Now you're making it sound like it's a goodbye."

"Not goodbye. Never goodbye. Always see you later." This was a lesson Katherine herself had always repeated to her only child.

Katherine had realized that Monica's happiness meant more to her than her own potential bragging abilities and nodded in agreement.

The Beginning

After convincing her mother to support her dreams (and graduating high school), Monica jumped into her van, which she had purchased off her deceased neighbor's children for twelve hundred dollars. There were over a hundred and fifty thousand miles on the van when she was handed its title, and by the time of her high school graduation, she had added another ten thousand driving to and from her school, listening to an eclectic playlist of songs recorded decades prior to her birth. Her peers would have laughed at this playlist and inquired as to whether or not it was actually music at all.

One of the most eccentric traits Monica possessed was her taste in music. She had often been made fun of for this preference, though she rarely opened her mouth to express her opinions in fear that the kids who sat in the back row of her classes making fun of the students that raised their hands would make fun of her as well. In reality, those 'teacher's pets' simply wanted the participation grade so their perfectionist, authoritarian parents would permit them to stay out past eight o'clock on Saturday nights.

One time, Monica overheard a war story in which the girl received a merciless punishment for getting stuck in traffic and missing her curfew by thirty seconds. Monica believed the girl had missed her curfew, but she seriously doubted she had only been less than a minute late. Monica understood it was human nature to exaggerate the truth for dramatics sake.

However, Monica herself tried to hold back the urge to use hyperbole to get her message across. This was especially true when Monica expressed her discomfort with some of the practices her teachers used to get students to participate in class to her mother, but Katherine continued to believe she was making a legend out of something inconsequential. Monica had never understood why the education system favored kids that were not too afraid of judgment to speak up.

The classes Monica felt most comfortable in were the ones where the teachers were not tempted to use their power to call on kids at random.

Monica often had nightmares in which the teacher decided they were tired of the same two kids answering all the questions. Monica would get picked to answer the hardest question and would then wake up drenched in sweat after what felt like days standing at the whiteboard, not even knowing how to start her response. She may have known the answer, but with all eyes on her, she froze.

As well as Monica knew herself, she did not care to make everyone aware of her stances. One of her biggest pet-peeves was when people started arguments for the sake of it, playing devil's advocate to get others riled up. However, if asked to express her opinion on a topic she was passionate about, she would happily give a thesisesque speech.

Monica had never been at the top of her class; in fact, she was a fairly average student. She was a naturally gifted thinker but was not interested in applying herself to topics she had no interest in. Instead of learning the cotton-eye joe, hot cross buns, or the quadratic formula, none of which she would use after graduation, she would have preferred to discuss the reason for living (that was a debate she longed to have).

The best grade Monica Lewis ever received was a ninety-nine in her philosophy class. The teacher was unable to bring himself to give her the credit she deserved. "No one gets a hundred in my class" were his words when Monica brought the grade book mistake to his attention.

The Saturday after Monica received a piece of paper reflective of twelve years of tears, fears, and worries, she set out on the road with a plan to travel until she felt the urge to stop. She also planned to immediately begin looking for a job; this was her top priority. She didn't care what the job entailed. Until then, however, she planned to live off the money she had saved while working at a department store, helping soccer moms find the manager to air their grievances.

She had worked a limited number of hours throughout her high school career (mostly only weekends) but kept everything she had earned tucked away in a bank account. Except for an occasional coffee, the only substantial purchase Monica had made was the van, which rolled off the factory floor a year before Monica herself.

After the death of Monica and Katherine's beloved neighbor, who would often make the trip across the cracked street to catch himself up on Monica's development, Monica decided she would help the neighbor's children, who never once, at least not that Monica could remember, showed up for Christmas dinner, by taking the vacant van off their hands.

This neighbor was beside Katherine and her mother when Monica took her first steps. He shed a tear or two when Monica first started kindergarten, watching her walk onto the school bus wearing the sparkly pink backpack that Katherine had picked off the shelf at the department store Monica would end up working at.

The neighbor had been the only constant male figure in Monica's life, and for that, Katherine was grateful. He brought a present across the street for the first sixteen of Monica's birthdays. He had hoped he would one day see Monica experience all of life's most significant milestones.

When they learned that this man had died of a stroke one night alone in his Massachusetts home, Monica and Katherine were devastated. They even went so far as to reach out to the man's negligent children, who were almost unfazed by their father's death. The youngest son, when told the tragic news about his father's passing, simply replied "who?"

Katherine had never understood why someone's children would abandon the person that gave them life as this man's children had abandoned him, and she promised herself that she would never let her relationship with her daughter deteriorate into a hostile text chain of "Happy Birthday" and "Thanks" twice a year.

The children, who had children of their own that were completely unaware of their grandfather's existence, were desperate to get rid of all traces of their father (when they eventually passed themselves, no one living would know he had ever existed), and Monica did the only thing she could to make sure that her neighbor would be remembered.

When Monica drove away from the only neighborhood she had ever known the day after she finished her formal education, she took a part of him with her.

The Writer

After deciding her final destination would be the Atlantic coast of the Sunshine State, Monica left her mother and everything she had ever known behind.

She stopped at a gas station around the corner from the house that was once the center of her universe to fill her gas tank and buy a can of soda for the ride. This was the last time her debit card was used in her home state.

She planned to make a handful of stops on the way to her once-thought impossible dream of independence, mostly to eat and use the bathroom. She also planned to spend a night, or two, depending on how fast she wanted to drive, in a cheap, roadside motel. She made special care to keep track of every dollar she was spending, hoping she wouldn't exhaust her limited funds too quickly.

After an hour cruising down the turnpike at a comfortable seventy miles an hour, she pulled off the road at a rest stop. She had already finished listening to nearly all of the songs on her favorite playlist, and it was during her walk to the women's bathroom that she regretted not downloading more music before she embarked on the slippery slope of a limited data plan.

After deciding she would take the time to curate a new eclectic mix of songs and artists at the next chance she got, she was approached by a young woman wearing skinny jeans, a black vest, and white sneakers. Monica had seen this woman from across the parking lot and took note of the frizzy nature of her short brown hair and the oily look of her pale and freckled face. Even with all this taken into account,

Monica noted that she didn't look dirty or neglected. In fact, Monica unconsciously compared this woman to a once-loved teddy bear she had not thought of in years. This woman, standing at no more than five-foot-three, guessed Monica, was not one to be afraid of.

"Hi," said the woman. Monica smiled back and nodded, surprised that someone would take the time to say hello. Typically, wherever she went she was ignored by people that thought she was too young to bother paying any attention to. When she walked down the street, strangers nodded at her mother and looked the other way when she passed. When leaving a restaurant, the host would wish her mother a good night but not her. She often wondered at what age adults began to think kids are worthy of a simple smile and nod.

"Hi." Right before she passed the woman, Monica got the feeling she did not intend to share only simple pleasantries.

"I don't mean to be forward," was the way she started. Monica was intrigued but had watched enough movie trailers and television show advertisements to know this might not end the way Monica hoped it would. "There's not a chance you would give me a ride, is there? I'm not a creep or anything like that; I just don't have anyone to drive me."

Monica was taken aback by the offer, an interested half-smile crossing over her face.

"Which way are you going?" The woman seemed surprised she had gotten a response.

"South."

"What's the destination?"

"As far as you'll take me."

Monica eyed the small-framed woman for a moment and decided she trusted herself more than whoever the next person the woman approached would have been. She, after only a handful of shared words, took it upon herself to protect this woman from the other people she imagined offered rides to young women at rest stops.

"Okay," was all Monica said for a moment. Monica had not yet determined how many trips around the sun the woman had made, but eventually settled on the large range between fifteen, which would explain the need for a ride, and late twenties, thirty at the most. She had an ageless face.

"Really?" The woman's tone combined a strange mix of gratefulness and bewilderment.

"Yeah, sure. Why not? What's your name?"

"Tessa," replied the woman. Monica reacted by subtracting a couple of years from her estimate; she couldn't imagine a Tessa being much older than herself. "What about you?"

"Monica."

"Monica. Nice to meet you. That was my aunt's name."

"Really?" Tessa shook her head affirmatively, smiling brightly. Monica now guessed she was at most twenty-five. "I've never met a Tessa."

"Neither have I, actually; I'm the first one I've met too."

The new friends shared their first laugh.

"Do you want to wait in the car? I just gotta go to the bathroom real quick." Tessa responded to Monica's offer with a look of confusion.

"I mean, I appreciate the trust, but I'm not sure you really want a total stranger sitting in your car. I mean, I know I said I wasn't, but I could totally be trying to kidnap you or something." Monica smiled. She was definitely younger than twenty-five.

"That right there is proof enough." Tessa shrugged her shoulders. "But I guess you're right"

Tessa nodded. "I'll wait here."

"Okay. I'll be right back." Monica walked into the bathroom.

Four minutes later, she walked out to find Tessa standing in the exact spot she left her.

"I didn't move." Tessa squinted one eye closed, blocking the fading sunlight from her vision with the palm of her hand.

Monica laughed and led Tessa back to the van.

After a few minutes of starting, yielding, and speeding to catch up with the flow of traffic in silence, Monica worked up the courage to ask Tessa, who was staring out the window at the landscape, supporting her head in her palm, how old she was.

"Twenty-four," was her answer as she turned to look at her chauffeur. "What about you?"

"Eighteen."

"Really?"

"Yeah." Monica took her eyes off the road for a minute.

"You seem older than that."

"That's what everyone's always told me."

"Where are you going?" It was Tessa's turn to ask the questions.

"Honestly, I don't really know. I mean, as of right now, it's Miami-"

"Oh wow."

"Yeah, but I'm not sure that's where I'll stay."

"What are you going to do there?"

"That's a great question." Monica let out a nervous laugh. As confident as she had been in her ability to evade the norm, she had no idea what her next step should be. "What about you?" Monica was in desperate need of suggestions.

"Oh, I know what I'm gonna do there." Both Monica and Tessa laughed. Tessa's smile faded as Monica focused her attention back on the highway. "I mean, I don't know how successful I'll be, but."

"Tell me about it."

"I don't think that's what life's about-"

"That's what I've said."

"Yeah. I guess it's more about finding the joy in the little things, you know."

"What do you do?" asked Monica.

"I'm a writer. Yeah. I was originally going to be a lawyer, but... I mean, that's what I had wanted to be. My teammates in high school and my parents and just basically everyone said I'd be a good lawyer. I think I would have been, but I started writing in high school, and I was super into drama. Like, pretty much everything I wrote had a cop in it, and somebody got arrested, and all that fun stuff. So, obviously, to make it more believable and everything I had to actually kind of understand the legal system. I mean, I didn't have to be an expert or anything. My philosophy is as long as it's believable, I can bend the truth a little bit to fit my purposes; everyone does, but the more I researched, the more upset I got. The system's completely broken, and it was designed to work that way. Like, there are people walking the streets right now that are a danger to the general population. They planned whatever they did, they talked about it, they prepared everything to do it, and they actually did it. Like, that takes a lot of planning, and there are so many opportunities to bail out, but nope, they wanted to do it. Then there are other people, and this is what honestly makes me even madder: people that just messed up, made a mistake, and are paying ridiculously for it. The punishments rarely fit the crimes. I'm terrified of like, even being pulled over now, I've freaked myself out so much because the punishments are so harsh, and I'm a small white woman. I can't imagine the absolute fear other people have to live in. It's insane. You can serve years and years and years for a first-time, nonviolent offense. It's ridiculous. A lot of people, who, by the way, are costing taxpayers millions, shouldn't have gotten half of what they did. Why are we letting people that are literal menaces to society roam the streets when we keep other people, oh my god, don't even get me started on the wrongly convicted, people that just got caught up in a bad situation, made some mistakes...they're suffering immensely now: why? I don't know, maybe it's just me being terrified of the legal system, but I know I couldn't do that personally. I get caught with a little, teeny-tiny bit of weed in some states, off to jail. You can't recover from that. That follows you for the rest of your life. It's ridiculous. I didn't want to be like a patent lawyer or anything like that, that just sounds kind of boring, and that's not what people picture when they think of lawyers, but I don't think I could live with myself if I had a hand in causing a morally good person that just 'misstepped' a little to go to jail, even if it was just like a month. I wouldn't be able to sleep at night. I don't want to be part of a system that is so flawed, unjust, and biased.

"I have this friend of a friend of a friend, we've met a couple of times; he was super nice and everything, and he really got screwed over. One night, he went out drinking with a couple of his friends, whatever, and after a while, they left. They were walking along the beach, I forget where it was, but I think they were on spring break or something, but the guy realized that he had to go to the bathroom, and being a little drunk, though I'm not sure you need any alcohol involved, he looked at the ocean and was like 'I'm just going to go there,' right? Everyone's done it. So whatever, he starts going to the bathroom, and a police officer that was patrolling the beach saw him, and now he's a registered sex offender. He's a night janitor with a Ph.D. in astrophysics."

"Oh my god." Monica looked over at an impassioned Tessa, who sat in angry silence, glaring at the highway in front of them.

"It just makes me so mad, you know?"

"Oh yeah. My mom always said I would be a good lawyer too, but I never even thought of that."

"I truly believe there are only a couple of reasons people commit crimes. First of all, they have a serious mental illness that needs to be addressed. The last thing you should do with a person that just needs a little help is to lock them up by themselves in cages like animals. It's inhumane. It's unethical. It's supposed to be about rehabilitation not punishment, right?

"The second reason, which I think accounts for a large percentage of the criminal activity, is because people are stuck in an economic and societal system that doesn't allow them to move up the ladder, and the only option they have is to act out. Instead of treating people as inferior simply because they were unlucky enough to be born into a family without as much money as the families the system was built for, we should make sure that everyone is given the same opportunity. Instead of offering an adequate education to only the kids that are born into privilege, everyone should be given an equal chance at success, right? Isn't that what America is supposed to stand for? The system we have now basically suggests that the American dream is only applicable to kids of rich families. The fact that they're locking up people that stole prescriptions for their dying children cause they couldn't afford it otherwise says a lot about the flaws in not only the legal system but also the economic system and the societal pyramid, no? Because there is such a disparity in opportunity, the people who are born into poverty through no fault of their own become trapped. For some people, the only way they'll get a roof over their head, three square meals, or a sense of protection of sorts is if they're in jail. If they can find a way to evenly distribute education funds and opportunities, I can almost guarantee that the crime rates will drop significantly. I think it's that simple. By opening a school door, you're closing a prison door. If you're not mentally ill or stuck in the system, anything else is just an accident, and you shouldn't have to pay for that."

"I agree with you, I just think there's more," Monica replied.

"Okay. Let's hear it."

"The people that have so much privilege they think they can get away with anything. The legal system is so focused on blue-collar and petty crimes, the rich people can pretty much do whatever they want without any real consequences. The richest of the rich can con people out of millions and millions of dollars through laundering, fraud, and embezzlement and get nothing more than a slap on the wrist. They're not doing it out of necessity, they're doing it out of greed, which is completely immoral, in my opinion. I don't know how that should be handled because those people are just selfish and should have to pay for that.

"You also have to consider the people that are serial killers, terrorists, school shooters, those types. They obviously need serious medical attention if they commit a crime as horrific as that, but I'm not sure they're really equipped to assimilate back into society, even if they do get that help. Again, though, as you said, it shouldn't be about punishment, it should be about rehabilitation. Instead of using the legal system as a weapon against people they don't want to deal with (the homeless, the unemployed, the immigrants, the people of color, the refugees, the mentally ill, the nonconformists), they should be focusing on real crimes. Tell me why people are still in jail for marijuana possession when their states have legalized it. Tell me why people involved in victimless *crimes* are sitting in jail before they even get a trial because they can't post bail. Tell me why they take away a felon's right to vote but still make them pay taxes; that is, at heart, taxation without representation. Tell me why you take away children's fathers for simple drug possession and then belittle them because they never got a dad. Tell me why people can sit at home and drink alcohol or caffeine, but they can't smoke weed. I'll tell you why: it was criminalized so they didn't have to deal with the hippies. Crack and heroin were criminalized and funneled into communities so they could get rid of black people. At a certain point, it's not even about the crime anymore, it's about getting rid of people that aren't the perfect representations of what the people in power stand for: white straight patriarchy."

"That's an interesting point," Tessa said. "I never really thought about that before, but I think I have to agree with you."

"Yeah." They sat in silence for a moment, both staring straight ahead, contemplating the statements they had made.

"So what do you write about now?" Monica never had an interest in storytelling; in fact, she was forced to put down many a novel she would have enjoyed reading had the author not gotten too preachy. She couldn't stand flowery, exaggerated prose where the author was unable to avoid the urge to go off on a long, drawn-out tangent.

Monica was also never interested in putting her own opinions out into the world to be picked apart by a political faction. Monica did have clear ideas of what she wanted the world to look like but was not willing to go through the effort to get her beliefs published only to be overlooked by pompous people in up-scale book stores and high schoolers only motivated to finish reading because of their opinion-based authorial-intent essay deadline.

Tessa laughed slightly, looking down at her hands. She had one ring on her right middle finger, which had been bought as a pack of ten for nine-ninety-nine. Her black nail polish was peeling and flaking off onto the floor mat. Monica made a mental note to herself to shake out the mat once she left Tessa behind, though she still had no idea how much further she intended for Monica to take her.

"Just because I don't want to be involved in it in real life doesn't mean I still don't write about it."

"Crime?"

"Yeah. Well, right now, I'm kind of taking a break from that to write a more peaceful, PG novel, but after that, I'm going to go back to writing screenplays that are laced with..." Tessa debated the ending of her sentence for a moment. "Well, every vice my mother told me not to get involved in."

"Oh," Monica laughed slightly. She personally felt no urge to disregard her mother's wishes for her separation from vice, though she had enjoyed overhearing the horror stories and petty drama the girls of her high school lunch table got caught up in. Still, she doubted many of the things her 'best friends' said were nothing but gossip.

"Yeah. The one I'm doing next is kinda about a stalker, so that's fun."

"Is it a personal story?"

"No, not at all." Tessa was glad the grisly stories she told were simply products of her imagination, and Monica was also relieved to hear this.

"I don't really know where most of them come from cause my life's been pretty calm, with the exception of a few existential crises and intrusive thoughts, but I'm sure that's normal," Tessa added.

"What do you mean?" Monica asked, a hint of giddy excitement in her tone. This was a conversation Monica was genuinely intrigued by.

"I don't wanna freak you out or anything."

"No, please do."

"Okay. Well, maybe everyone you've ever met is just a product of your imagination."

"Oh." Monica had considered the possibility.

"Like, who's to say you're real? Who's to say I'm real? Maybe I'm only saying this because I was programmed to say this exact thing at this exact moment. Maybe you're only driving me because you have to. Your free will may be overridden by some higher power. I mean, when you really think about it, maybe we are just laying down in some futuristic coffin hallucinating all of this. Life is an illusion, a construct. I mean, the world is only the way it is because some powerful people sat down and decided that we were going to drive on the right side of the road, compete for nothing more than green pieces of paper, that skinny equates to superior, and that colors and skin pigments should divide the world. Why are we all so willing to accept what some white guy that's been dead for hundreds of years once wrote down as fact?"

"I can see what you're saying; we've been conditioned to just follow along," said Monica, a smile on her face. "And maybe we're here right now because we have to be. We don't have a choice. Maybe we're not even real."

"Exactly; everyone always says I'm crazy when I say these things, but I think we should at least ponder them, no? It only adds to the human experience."

"Totally. My mom just a few days ago was talking about how we have complete and total control over our own lives, and no amount of torture or interrogation or anything can make us give up information we don't want to, and I can see what's she's saying, but I think your argument's just as valid."

"I mean, are we even talking right now? Did you really see me at the rest stop and decide to pick me up? Am I even here with you? Are you even here? I sometimes have nightmares where I just wake up one morning and am five years old again and realize the miserable existence I thought was my life was all just an unconscious dream." Tessa took a deep breath and focused her attention on the side of Monica's head. "That terrifies me. I mean, why are we even here? What's our purpose? What separates me from you and us from the rest of the world? Not everyone is going to be the next big inventor, or mathematician, or even writer, for me. Why am I writing? What, one day, made me want to pick up a pen and put my own beliefs and theories into the direct line of fire of judgment? I know I'm not special, so what motivates me to get up in the morning? Is it because I don't have a choice?"

"I think to some extent we don't have a choice, but we can always work to try and improve. I believe in fate, and therefore, that everything we see, say, and do is going to happen to us no matter what decision we make. However, if you think that you can just float along in the world and let fate take over, you're not going to get that far, because your fate was simply to be lazy."

"Right!" Tessa was ecstatic to express her opinions for the first time in many years without being brushed aside and called irrational. The last time Tessa had experienced this, she was sitting in a bathtub trying to cut her favorite doll's hair and telling her mother she wanted to look just like the doll before the botched haircut: statuesque, blond, and beautiful. Her mother nodded, telling her she could be whatever she wanted, and though it may not have been the best response the tired and lost woman could have given to her young daughter, she had the right idea. She would spend the next ten years instructing her daughter on the dangers of drugs and premarital sex, which would inspire Tessa to write on those exact topics later in life, most likely inspired by some unconscious drive to spite her mother. She had nearly gotten disowned when she showed off her first tattoo: a snake wrapped around her pinky finger. Her mother, screaming in a blind fit of rage, asked Tessa how she thought she was ever going to get a job looking like *that*. Tessa got the first job she interviewed for without the help of any bandages, makeup, or gloves.

"You have to continuously work to get where you want in life, but that just means you were always supposed to be successful in the first place. I think people, in a sense, kind of do have the notion that they are in control of their own life, even though their decision in every moment may have been finalized before they were born, and that is comforting," Monica added.

"Laziness is what hurts people the most. Who are you without ambition? If you aren't taking the steps to get what you want, you're digging yourself into an even deeper hole. The lazier you become, the less you feel you'll be able to do, making you try even less later. It's a vicious cycle, I think," finished Tessa.

"I agree, and I think that's why some people are so eager to take the easy path in life and follow in the footsteps of all the trendsetters, even if those people didn't do anything remarkable themselves."

"People seem to have such high hopes for life," Tessa added passionately, her voice reverberating through the closed space. The windows were closed and the air conditioning was blowing lightly. "We make it out to be this magical, incredible thing, and then when people live a normal life, which is what most people live anyways, they're disappointed that they haven't done anything spectacular. We're setting a standard that every single moment you have to be studying quantum physics, or writing the next great American novel, or figuring out a more efficient way to start your microwave using solar power from your backyard.

Why can't we be satisfied simply watching television or singing poorly or dancing like one of those things outside of car dealerships or reading some obscure blog post? Why does society put pressure on everyone to be constantly doing something amazing, never taking the time to slow down and appreciate the little things?"

"That's literally what I've been saying my whole life. I was a decent student. I could have gone to college, gotten a *real* job, whatever that means, all that kind of stuff, but I wanted to live. I wanted to appreciate the little things, but I kept feeling the pressure to conform because that's what everyone else does."

"Peer-pressure is a powerful thing, bro." Tessa pulled her legs up onto the seat, tucking them under her body, perching herself on the faded-gray polyester like a bird in a nest. "That's good you didn't give in to it like I did."

"What do you mean?" Monica had been convinced she had found someone that shared her most *outlandish* beliefs. When thrown this curveball, she became genuinely confused. She thought becoming a crime writer was nothing to be embarrassed by, though she also thought nobody should be ashamed of their occupation, whether it be a job or a career.

"Well, I probably should have told you this first, but I actually just write on the side, which is fine with me, but I know that's not really what you were thinking."

"No, it's fine. It doesn't change my opinion," Monica claimed with a slight smile.

"I've never met someone like you."

"I'll take that as a compliment."

"You should," Tessa laughed.

"So what do you do then?" Monica shifted into the fast lane, trying to get around the semi-truck in front of them.

"I'm a high school English teacher, and I wait some tables on the side. I like it though."

"That's cool."

"Yeah. It makes me feel good about myself, at least a little bit, that I get paid to read the classics and hopefully inspire some kids to fall in love with writing the same way I did when I was their age. It saved my life, and I hope that I can help another teenager find that themself. Even if I don't ever get anything published, maybe I can encourage one of them to do what I couldn't. I've only taught one year so far, but I'm excited for more. Then I wait some tables so I can at least have some social stimulation with people my own age, cause without it, I would just lock myself in my apartment, turn all the lights off, and write, and then cry about how horrible of a writer I am. That's the funny thing about it; when you're writing you either think you're the stupidest, most illiterate fool to have ever lived or you're literally god. That's it. There's no in-between." Tessa and Monica both let out a laugh.

"That's good though, that you have something you're passionate about. I wish I had that; a lot of people don't. I know I want to live an interesting life, but I don't know how to get there." Monica took a deep breath, trying to gather her thoughts.

"You know, that seems to be a common consensus with the teenagers I had. They all wanted to do something extraordinary and be famous and rich, but they have no idea how to do that. It's normal. Don't worry about it."

Monica looked over at Tessa with a smile. "Yeah. I don't need to be rich or famous; I have no desire to be whatsoever."

"That makes it easier," Tessa added matter-of-factly.

"Yeah. I don't think my expectations are too high, I just wanna live, you know. I want to enjoy the ride?"

"So you really don't have a plan for when you get there?" Tessa, based on her tone, was genuinely interested in the minute details of Monica's future.

Monica looked out the window, her grip tightening on the steering wheel. She did not realize how white her knuckles had gotten; Tessa did and took note of this.

"It's all right. I'm sure you'll be fine. You just have to figure it out. In due time, it'll all make sense."

Monia nodded her head and smiled. She added a quiet, insecure "yeah."

What If We Woke Up?

The Gay Man

Monica Lewis left Tessa in the parking lot of a coffee shop somewhere in the middle of Connecticut. She continued down the highway for another half an hour before deciding to pull over and get something quick to eat at a gas station in the middle of farm country. She had never understood how people lived so far away from any other form of human life. She imagined it must get lonely, and although Monica herself was a rather reserved individual, she needed some contact with other people (in limited quantities, of course).

Monica also felt the need to be close to the ocean; she felt almost a vague hint of claustrophobia when she got too far away. That was why Miami had beat out Orlando as the final destination. Monica had, in the thirty minutes of solitude after Tessa's departure, officially settled on Miami.

When she reached the gas station, she purchased a pre-made turkey sandwich, which at that point was approaching four days since its original construction.

While stepping in line to pay, she was confronted by a lanky man wearing jeans and a gray sweater. He held an iced coffee in one hand and a cell phone in the other. His glasses slid off the bridge of his nose, and every so often, he was forced to reposition them. With every push of the brims, he became more distraught. Why should he have to pay to see when someone lucky enough to be born with normal vision gets to keep that money in their pocket, he wondered.

They both approached the line at the same time and offered each other the first position. After a laugh, Monica accepted and stepped in front of him, cradling the aged turkey sandwich close to her chest.

While waiting for the only other person in line to pay, Monica and the man, who was named James, began talking, and after a while (the other person took a long time to find a credit card that wasn't denied), Monica once again offered her passenger seat to a new friend.

After chatting and purchasing their dinners, they marched toward Monica's van.

Setting up camp in the driver's seat, Monica became interested in James' backstory. Why, she wondered, was he also at the gas station at the same time? Could it be, as Tessa had thought, he was there for a reason: to become a strong supporting side-character in the feature film that was Monica's life?

James, making himself comfortable in the seat beside Monica, thanked her for offering her services.

"No problem. Where are you headed?" asked Monica. They had earlier established that they were intending to go in the same direction but had not gotten specific.

"I'm goin' home. It's my aunt's birthday, so we're gonna celebrate her. Have some cake. Open some presents."

"Oh, that's fun," Monica added earnestly.

"Yes. I'm excited. They're meeting my boyfriend for the first time, so I'm a little nervous, but."

"Oh my god, that's so exciting." Monica carried out the "-ing" much longer than she should have.

"Yes. But enough about me; what about you, girl?"

"Me?"

What If We Woke Up?

"Of course. Who else?" Monica laughed at this.

"No, I just...no one's ever said that."

"There's a first time for everything."

"So I've heard."

"Well?" James waited expectantly, slurping his coffee. Monica kept her eyes on the road, debating her response.

"I'm going to Miami, actually."

"Really?" James looked at Monica enthusiastically. "That's exciting."

"Yeah, I am excited," Monica said with an assertiveness she did not truly feel. "Now it's your turn. You tell me something." Monica looked over at James, smiling warmly.

"Oh honey, I don't know where you wanna start."

"Tell me about your boyfriend."

"If I start I'm not gonna stop." Monica laughed.

"That's all right. My life's pretty boring anyway; you don't really wanna hear about it."

"All lives are exciting."

"In their own way, I suppose," Monica shrugged.

"Exactly. Okay. So." James straightened his posture, so much so that his back was no longer touching the seat. "His name's Michael, and he's like super hot." Both Monica and James chuckled for a moment. "Like, for real, for real. He works out like every day, which is insane, right?"

"Oh, gross. That doesn't sound fun."

"Not for him, but for me," James added a passionate "whew," throwing his hands up in the air.

63

Monica began to take the wrapper off her sandwich, half expecting to be met with green and blue bread and a musty smell. Monica had stopped reading the label after "turkey," which was the first listed, and hoped she hadn't overlooked any ingredients she didn't like. The wrapper came off after a single tug on the masking tape, and Monica examined it, looking for any hint of souring.

"That literally smells like a farm." James eyed the sandwich himself, suspicious of its quality.

After letting out a light laugh, Monica added: "Yeah, but it was four dollars." She undid the rest of the wrapper. "So he's never met your family?"

"No. Actually, I've never brought a guy home."

"Oh my god." Monica's eyes widened.

"I know. I'm like super scared. They didn't even know for a while, so like, that makes it even worse, you know. I don't think it would have been that hard to figure out, but no one said anything so. It was always 'James, when are you gonna bring your girlfriend home?' and all that kind of stuff. Like, grandma, I'm not bringing a girl home. Are you blind?" James brought his hand up to his face, covering his mouth. "Oop. She's just deaf."

"Is she gonna be there?" The sandwich tasted just as bad as it smelled.

"Yeah, everyone is."

"Oh," Monica responded with a nervous laugh.

"Yeah. Well, except for my dad."

"How come?"

"We've..." James looked out the windshield and cleared his throat. "We've never really gotten along. I don't know, we were always arguing. I felt like he wanted so much from me; he wanted me to do everything he never could, and I'm not superhuman, you know?"

"Totally. I think a lot of parents wanna be able to brag that their kids got the life they didn't."

"But then suddenly," James added, "you get older, and they realize you don't serve them any purpose anymore. When they first have kids, they read all the books, they do all the things they're supposed to do. Nobody reads books about teenagers or kids that have outgrown their cuteness or don't want to right the parent's wrongs. Then they'll start to think anytime you voice an opposing opinion you're looking to fight, that you're being moody and irrational."

"Exactly."

"That's I think where it all started to go downhill. He realized I wasn't the person he imagined me being and started to give me the impression that everything I was doing was wrong. So, naturally, I stopped telling him things. One day he said something about some celebrity he watched on tv coming out, I don't even remember who it was, but I just went to my room and started crying. I had never felt so misunderstood, you know. That's when I realized how lonely the world really is. I think I was like ten or eleven. I was in elementary school crying because my father had made a comment degrading something that was a part of me I had no control over, a part of me that I couldn't deny, so I never told him. Even if I had wanted to, I wouldn't have known how."

"The hardest thing is knowing you're not accepted for being who you are. There's nothing you can change about it, and I think that's what a lot of people don't understand. They didn't wake up one morning and say 'you know what, I think I'm straight,' so why do they think anyone else does?"

"Yeah."

"Did other people know?"

"I never directly said anything, but I think people nowadays, even if they don't support it, which is much more common than you'd think, know what it *should* look like, even though it's different for everyone. They're always looking out for it. They'll whisper about it. 'Do you think he's...you know...one of *them*?' putting special emphasis on the 'them' of course, making sure that everyone around knows that they're not one of 'them'; they'd rather die than be a part of *that* group. It makes me really mad when people are like 'oh, I support the gays and all, but I could never do that. That's disgusting. I don't get how they could do it.' They pretend they're cool with it and then go and make some backhanded statement that makes it sound like the mother of all sins."

"If people were slower to judge and just minded their own business, life would be a lot more enjoyable for everyone. I mean, why should it matter what the person passing you on the sidewalk does in their personal life? You're never going to meet them, you're never going to talk to them, so the only person that you're hurting is yourself, getting your blood pressure up to the point that you give yourself a heart attack after so many years of worrying about other people's personal business."

"That's what I've been saying, honey." James took a deep breath. "That's pretty much why I never told him."

"It's awful." Monica had always been passionate about the ingroup's intolerance for the outgroup.

"A couple of years ago, I had come home for the holidays from school, and we were all just sitting on the couch, watching a movie, eating cake, all that stuff. It was me, my parents, brother, sister, and cousin, and we were having a good time. I wasn't super stressed, which was unusual because I'm always worried about something-"

"That's relatable."

"Yeah, but we were just chillin' watching the tv, and one of the characters turned out to be gay himself. So, naturally, I kind of looked down and pretended to be interested in the couch. I wasn't embarrassed or anything, well not when I was away from them, but that's when my dad made another comment. I don't even remember what he said, but my cousin, wanting to stick up for me cause he thought everyone knew, turned around and said something to my dad like 'don't say that when James's here.' I'll never forget the way my father looked at me." Monica shook her head and sighed.

"He started screaming, and I remember watching his cake fall off his plate and onto the floor when he stood up and threw a pillow at me before storming off. Nobody said anything for a couple of minutes, they all just kind of sat there uncomfortably. The movie kept playing. It was the laugh track that got me, just the irony of it all. I was sitting down beside my closest relatives, the people I should have been supported most by, listening to laughing in the background, feeling completely alone and lost. That was the worst moment of my life." By this point, Monica's eyes began filling with tears. She kept her fingers clasped tightly around the wheel, whitening her knuckles even further.

"We haven't really talked since then. I don't know what to say. I don't think I should have to apologize-"

"No. Not at all."

"I don't know what to do. He refuses to even text me back now."

"I know this isn't what you're looking for, but if he wants to act like an idiot, it's his loss. He shouldn't be so ignorant that he can't accept his son isn't the mirror image of himself."

James shifted in the seat to look at Monica, who was squinting against the ever falling sun. He smiled kindly. There was a lightness in his eyes that Monica was unaccustomed to seeing on anyone other than her own reflection, but his did not go much deeper than the surface. Although his mouth was curled upwards, there was a visible pain in his gaze.

"Thanks. I really appreciate it."

"Sure." Monica took her eyes off the road for a moment to look at James. "I'm sure it'll go great tonight."

"Oh, of course it will. When I say he's hot, he's hot." Both Monica and James laughed.

What If We Woke Up?

The Runner

James politely requested that Monica leave him at the next rest stop they passed, and after seeing a sign advertising for one, Monica and James pulled off the highway and parted ways, never to speak again.

James's fears regarding the introductory meeting of his boyfriend and his family spread their seeds deeper into James's racing heart as the minutes passed.

James was unaware that his estranged father was in fact planning to take part in the celebration. He arrived at the gathering earlier than James, and when he saw his eldest son walk through the front door beside a muscular man, his years of ignorance and frustration manifested themselves all at once.

However, before James even left the rest stop, not knowing what the rest of his day held, Monica walked into a bathroom for the second time that day.

When she walked out of the building, James was no longer standing in the parking lot. Monica smiled to herself, hoping his evening would go according to plan; it would not.

On the walk across the parking lot back to the van, humming to herself, swinging her keychain, trying to work out her sleeping arrangements, watching the sun dip deeper into the horizon, she noticed a man pulling himself out of the shadows of the woods beside the building. Monica, caught off guard, did the one thing she subconsciously knew she should not do; she stopped and stared at the man, an expression of bewilderment crossing over her face.

The man stood up and dusted off his jeans.

He, wearing a faux leather jacket and a white t-shirt, stretched his arms above his head, sore after a long walk.

From Monica's point of view, he looked like he had just woken up, and his yawning only perplexed her more. She was so confused that she continued watching, a look of puzzlement over her face, long after she knew she should have looked away. She considered for a moment whether the man looked like he needed assistance, but he seemed content with his situation.

The man scratched his head, and Monica began to walk back to her van, hoping he would not pose a danger to himself or the other people at the rest stop.

Her sudden movement caught the man's attention, his eyes filling with an odd mix of panic and thankfulness. He jogged in Monica's direction.

Monica and Isaiah, as it turned out the man was named, sat in the front seats of Monica's van. They spent the first few minutes of their relationship speeding down the highway in awkward silence.

Isaiah took off his jacket, dropping it onto the floor beneath him, collecting Tessa's abandoned nail polish in the faux leather. Monica had not shaken out her mat.

She was still confused as to what Isaiah was doing hauling himself out of the woods alongside a freeway at dusk and wasn't sure she wanted to know.

"This is awkward," Isaiah started. He didn't care for small talk, but for whatever reason, something inside him said it would be comical if he commented on the state of their budding bond.

"A little bit." Monica kept her eyes on the road. "Can I ask you a question?"

"Finally. It took you long enough." Monica was unsure of what this meant.

"Why were you in the woods?" Isaiah looked at Monica for a moment, pondering his answer. His face scrunched up as he considered.

"Oh, you know," Isaiah answered after a long pause.

"Right. Of course."

"I sense some sarcasm there," he added, a hint of aggravation in his tone.

"Me? Not at all."

"Okay, well now I *know* it's there," Isaiah moaned.

"Maybe if you told me-"

"Just leave it alone. It doesn't matter."

"Whatever. I just woulda felt better if I knew you weren't trying to kill me or something."

"Maybe I am."

"Well, then you're not gonna get very far." Monica's pitch went up an octave.

Isaiah slumped down in his seat, crossing his arms and pouting. Under any other circumstance, Monica would have laughed at the child-like nature of his appearance. Instead, she focused on the road ahead of her, keeping her peripheral vision focused on Isaiah, who looked more like an elementary school child than a man. She guessed he was probably in his mid-thirties, and this only confused Monica more. If he had been younger, Monica guessed she would have been less disturbed by their original encounter.

She stared at the dashed lines dividing the lanes of the highway as they flashed past her. It made her dizzy to watch them, so she forced herself to look away, focusing on the bumpers of the cars in front of her.

The last thing Monica needed (or could afford) was having to pay for expensive repairs, the costs of which were only determined after the mechanic calculated how easily he could take advantage of the customer. Monica was not an imposing person nor did she possess any real knowledge on mechanics and therefore knew she would have gotten ripped off.

Isaiah sat up a bit stiffer in his seat, focusing his gaze out the window, the back of his head to Monica.

The only thing he truly desired was a confidant. He wanted someone he could talk to honestly. He was a talkative and friendly person by nature and had enjoyed his time working as a telemarketer and then later as a salesman, but he desired a deeper connection. Isaiah had had a series of girlfriends throughout his life, mostly stemming from his college days, but as thankful he was for the time spent with each of them, he desired a more intimate and trusting relationship.

Isaiah had been popular in his glory days but had never really felt he had true friends. His best friend had better best friends, and he often found himself scrolling through pictures of them at events he wasn't invited to. Even though he did have a few people he was close to, he wanted only to be able to let out his innermost feelings without being scrutinized or called names historically used to degrade women.

He was a sensitive man, but the world had convinced him that a real man never cried (or expressed any true feelings at all, except for hunger and lust).

If Isaiah had grown up in a world where there was no judgment for being honest and no definition of manliness, he would have turned out very differently than the man that sat beside an apprehensive Monica and the man his older brother had curated.

Isaiah's brother was ten years older than he was and was like a father-figure to him. He had taught Isaiah what a *real man* looked, acted, and sounded like. His brother desired to turn him into an exact replica of himself; he thought he perfectly fit the definition of manliness.

When Isaiah moved into an apartment of his own, he spent every single night crying himself to sleep. He would sleep for six or, if he was lucky, seven hours a night but lied in bed for a total of twelve every single day.

He could not bring himself to drag his aching and tired body out of the comfort of his bed every morning to face his brother's constant, incessant, and unrealistic expectations.

His nights would typically end with him in the fetal position on the hardwood floor struggling to breathe. He would then, still winded, crawl over to his mattress, which sat in the middle of the room, and pull a single blanket over his increasingly bony body, shaking not from the cold of another lonely winter night but instead from his brother's expectations for Isaiah's life.

Isaiah was partially convinced that his brother was understanding enough to loosen his grip over Isaiah's life if they had a simple face-to-face conversation, but Isaiah had never been taught to express his feelings. He felt that anytime he got close to truly explaining the inner workings of his brain, he would either be silenced by external factors, or he would shut down internally right before the climax. Every meaningful conversation Isaiah intended to have left him with a bitter taste in his mouth. With every word, he became more and more convinced that he should never have started talking in the first place.

Isaiah had intended to eventually find a way to express his thoughts to his brother and had spent his evenings, in between increasingly shallow breaths, searching the internet for tips on how to be less nervous and more honest. He also secretly hoped this would aid him in his quest to find the perfect woman to listen to his thoughts, placing her hand on his chest and her head on his shoulder, always attentive and occasionally pausing to add suggestions and solutions.

This was what he thought about when he wasn't preoccupied with his brother's forecast for his life, which wasn't very often. Isaiah had built a facade to hide behind, but its foundation was not as strong as Isaiah pretended it was. With a single blow of the wind, it would have come toppling over, crushing Isaiah and all aspects of his life, which was written, directed, and produced by his older brother.

Everywhere Isaiah went, his brother went with him. Everywhere Isaiah wanted to go, his brother unintentionally mocked and demeaned. His brother did have Isaiah's best interests at heart but was unable to understand that Isaiah's wishes could have differed from his own at all.

Isaiah felt stifled by his brother, and, as they aged, they continued to grow further apart. Although the two men appeared almost inseparable to outsiders, they were not close. Any chance that they could develop a relationship was murdered when Isaiah's brother introduced him to the concept of manliness.

Isaiah tried to tell his brother the truth time and time again but was unable to string together the correct words to convey the meaning he wished. This, coupled with his inability to make any progress in the professional areas of his life and difficulty in finding a suitable partner, led Isaiah to many sleepless nights.

However, there was a certain aura surrounding Monica that Isaiah seemed convinced invited conversation.

He loosened his arms, relaxed his shoulders, and turned to look forwards, the back of his head no longer facing Monica, who herself felt, for reasons she could not describe, he was on the verge of a breakthrough.

Looking at the road ahead, Isaiah whispered: "I was running."

Monica turned to look at Isaiah, her grip on the steering wheel loosening.

"What?" Monica asked. Isaiah had begun to speak so softly that Monica could only have guessed he had spoken.

"I was running." This time, Isaiah said it with an assertiveness that surprised even him as he shifted to face Monica.

"You were running." Monica was unsure of what this meant.

"Yeah."

"Like, jogging?"

"No, no. I was running from something. Someone. Everyone." Isaiah's voice cracked slightly; Monica was paying close enough attention to take note of this.

"Anything in particular?" Monica took her eyes off the road momentarily.

"I guess." Isaiah began to fiddle with his fingers.

"You wanna tell me?" Monica's tone invited one of the few things Isaiah had wished for: conversation. Real, true, meaningful conversation.

"I don't know."

"All right." Monica assumed he would eventually give in.

He did when he added: "my brother."

"Can I ask why?"

"I guess you could." Monica blew a puff of air out of her nose, expressing her amusement.

"He just..." Isaiah took a deep breath. "He just wants something I can't give him. He expects so much from me, and I don't have some magic ability to get everything he wants. I'm not who he wants me to be, and I don't think either of us gets that. I just wanna live my own life and make my own decisions and do things that I wanna do, not because he tells me I have to." Monica nodded her head, coming to the conclusion that they were not so different after all.

"That," Monica added, "I understand."

"Really?" Isaiah, for the first time in recent memory, truly believed that someone could empathize with his life's struggles.

The ironic part of this was that many people could relate to him but were too afraid to let their insecurities manifest themselves in the form of words or visible emotions. Isaiah would come to believe that the reason the world is such a lonely place is because tradition stressed the importance of struggling in the shadows, never showing any real emotion. "Real men never cry" was the lesson Isaiah had been taught over the course of his life, and therefore, he bottled up all inner battles, which would later become unavoidable when he lied down on his apartment floor, struggling to breathe, and started to sob, quietly at first, and ending with a finale of dry heaves and an encore of partial suffocation. The after-party included dizziness and a complete detachment from reality, which was what scared Isaiah the most; he had no idea how real the world, or he for that matter, was. He would wake up with a hangover and feel the effects for the rest of the day while preparing himself for the next night's show.

He never informed his brother of his late night and early morning performances and, even if he wanted to, he had no idea how to begin explaining his all-consuming struggle.

Isaiah had convinced himself that his brother, who was a decent person himself, would perceive him differently if he told him he was not okay.

His brother, as understanding as he may have been, seemed to hold onto an out-dated belief. To be convinced that someone was struggling, he needed a cast, an x-ray, or a pair of crutches. He did not understand that some people were fighting constant battles against themselves and were losing badly.

"Completely," Monica added with a smile. "I think most people do, even if they're too afraid to say it."

"It just..." Isaiah shook his head side-to-side. "It just consumes me. That's all I can think of: not letting him down, and I don't know how to tell him that. I don't want him to get all defensive and think that I'm blaming him, I just..." Isaiah's voice cracked again. "I just want a hug." For the first time in many years, Isaiah began to cry in the presence of another person.

The last time Isaiah had committed such a "sin" he was six years old. He was riding his bicycle, which still had training wheels on it, when a twig sent him over the handlebars. Luckily, he had been wearing a helmet and was left with a mild concussion and a few scratches. Being too young to attend first grade, he began to cry for his brother. He was more concerned with the sight of his blood staining his white sleeves than anything else.

His oldest brother, who had been riding in front of him, turned around, and instead of offering the helping hand young Isaiah needed, he walked over to him and took the opportunity to equip Isaiah with one of life's most *valuable* lessons. He, over the tears and pouting lips, told Isaiah that if he wanted to be taken seriously, if he wanted to be a *big boy*, he should never cry. Never, not once.

Isaiah looked up to his brother like a son would look up to his father and therefore stopped the waterfall that came

79

from his eyes and "sucked it up." That's what his brother had told him to do.

He didn't cry when he fell out of a tree and broke his arm three years later. He didn't cry when his mother went to bed one night and didn't wake up. He didn't cry when he went to live with his brother, sister-in-law, and nephew. He only cried when he was in the company of the people he was most comfortable with: himself and only himself (although even then he felt out of place).

He was surprised when his eyes began to water in front of a teenage girl he had just met.

When Monica reached across the middle console and patted Isaiah lightly on the shoulder, he finally broke down.

"It's all right," Monica added in an almost whisper.

"It's not." Isaiah was fighting back tears.

"No, it is. Why wouldn't it be?"

"I'm sorry."

"You don't have to say sorry. What do you have to be sorry for?"

"I..." Isaiah faded out, taking a deep breath and wiping his nose. "I don't know."

"I'll try not to judge you." Isaiah's whimpers were momentarily replaced by a light laugh.

"Promise?"

Monica paused to truly weigh her options. This confused Isaiah even more. He had never met a person that took the time to carefully choose each word, making sure they were conveying the meaning they intended to. This was something Monica did with every sentence. In this case, after carefully considering her options, she concluded that she would not benefit in any way from judging him.

"Yeah, I promise," Monica added.

"I don't know where to start."

"Wherever you want. Once you get going, it'll probably be easier."

"Is that how it works?" Isaiah turned his moist face to Monica, who looked back, nodding affirmatively.

"I'm not used to..." Isaiah didn't even know where to begin explaining his inexperience with conversation. "Well, I don't know what I'm not used to; I don't know what's normal."

"Go for it. Try me. I'm all ears."

"I don't even know you," Isaiah uttered in a tone Monica could only have described as heartfelt and caring.

"I'm not sure I know myself either." Isaiah pointed a bony finger at Monica and wagged it.

"That's a good place to start," he said.

"All right. Let's hear it."

"Well, I don't know. If..." Isaiah found his aversion to expressing himself diminishing by the second. He sat back in Monica's passenger seat comfortably and smiled.

"I was running from my brother." A feeling of relief washed over him. "I hate him. I hate him, but I love him. He's always been...well, nice to me. He's always done the little things, you know. He baked me cakes for my birthdays, even though he can't cook. He bought me a car for my sixteenth birthday, he always gave me the window seat, he took me to the movies and amusement parks, and he coached my baseball team. He let me live out of his spare bedroom, he made me the godfather of his son; I was the best man at his wedding. I love him. The reason I am who I am today is because he raised me, but I hate myself. I'm grateful for everything he's done, but sometimes I can't help thinking that I would have been better off being truly alone. I didn't want the life he chose for me, and I still don't. He got me a job with him, but I never wanted that. I wanted to get a real job. I wanted to sit in an office and go home and ask my children how their school day was and then spoil my wife when they went to bed. I wanted to drive the minivan; I wanted to coach my own son's baseball team if he wanted to play. I wanted to live in the suburbs, have the white picket fence, and compete with my neighbors for the nicest lawn. I didn't want to always answer to him. That's not the worst part though. If I were a normal person, I would have told him that; I would have told him that years ago. I'd probably have the life I wanted by now, but, for whatever reason, I can't stand up for myself. I don't want to let him down; I really don't. He had such high hopes for me, and I think he still does, but I'm not sure, well I know, I'm not cut out for the life he wants me to live. I'm so afraid to let him down, I let him control every aspect of my life to the point that I'm not even sure it's mine anymore. I love him, but I hate me." Isaiah turned to look at Monica. "Is that weird?"

"Not at all," Monica added genuinely. "I think we've all kinda felt the same way at some point, but you know what?"

"What?" Isaiah asked with a sniffle.

"You still have plenty of life to live. What you're doing now isn't what you're always going to be doing. I've always found it ironic that people say they wouldn't want to time travel to the past because they'd be so scared they'd change something, but no one thinks they can change the future while living in the present." Isaiah pondered this. "I promise you, it will get easier. It's hard right now, of course it is, but once you start being honest, you're not gonna want to stop. If you tell him now, everything could change. He'd understand, and you'd sleep easier. It doesn't mean he'd automatically agree, but knowing has to be better than constantly wondering, no? I didn't tell my mother what I truly wanted for a while because I was scared of what she was going to say, but I can tell you now I feel a whole lot better, and I'm doing what I want to do. She may not have been happy, and I doubt she ever will be, but it's my life, not hers. Unfortunately for your brother, he only got one life; yours isn't his." Isaiah began picking the dirt out from under his fingernails.

"I'm not gonna go back." Monica looked at Isaiah, who stared off into the distance, his eyes wet.

If he told his brother he believed it would become almost too real: there would be no turning back. "I was running from him forever. I can't face him. I'm not strong enough to." Monica shook her head in dissonant understanding (she thought anyone was strong enough, no matter the situation). "I'm not going back. I'm never going back. I just ran away, disappeared off the face of the Earth."

"When'd you start running?"

"This morning."

"And have you thought it over?"

"Yeah. You know what, I have. Because I was either going to run or put a gun to my head. I'm glad I chose to run. I do want to live, just not the life I had been living. I'm gonna end up somewhere, I'm gonna meet a nice girl, I'm gonna have a family, and when I do eventually die of natural causes, I'm not gonna regret anything, all right?" Monica smiled and shook her head once.

"All right with me."

"Yeah. That's what I'm gonna do." Isaiah's tears had transitioned to blind passion.

'Good for you."

"That's what I'm gonna do, and if he has a problem with it, I'm not gonna worry about it. He's not my problem anymore."

"Sounds like a plan to me. Do you think you'll ever tell him?" Isaiah's shoulders sank.

"I hadn't thought about that. I think I have to. I owe it to him. I'll tell him I just had to go, then I'll explain it later. I think if I'm not face-to-face with him, it'll be a little easier. I won't have to look him in the eye. I've never been good at that." Isaiah stared out the front windshield at the road ahead. It had gotten so dark, the headlights from other cars were the only signals that they were not completely alone on the road.

Monica was growing increasingly tired and fought to keep her eyes open. She knew she, for the safety of both herself and all other drivers on the road, should pull over, but had no idea what to do with Isaiah, who she did not want to leave alone. For the second time that day, Monica felt that she was protecting another person by offering her gas and polyester seat.

"It's getting late," Monica finally noted aloud.

"Yeah. Do you plan on sleeping?"

"I don't know. I don't think I can really afford a motel room. What were your plans?" Monica asked. She was once again in need of suggestions.

"I was just gonna lay down when I got tired." Monica laughed; Isaiah was serious.

"Well, that doesn't help," Monica said.

"Yeah, I guess not." Monica turned around momentarily and looked behind her. The van had a few feet of cargo space behind the front seats. Monica's neighbor had emptied the back to make space for the equipment he had needed for his job.

"How tall are you?" Monica asked.

Isaiah, perplexed, answered after a moment. "Five-eleven. I usually round it up a little, but I don't think I need to lie anymore. Why are you asking?"

After pulling off the highway at the next exit, Monica, with Isaiah's help, located the nearest department store and parked the van on the outskirts of its lot. They had come to the mutual agreement that they both would rest in the back of the van. She understood clearly that Isaiah would have stopped and slept wherever he started to feel drowsy and wanted to prevent the hassle that would have accompanied being awoken by well-meaning citizens or law enforcement officers.

The pair climbed into the back of the van and lied down. Before drifting off to sleep, Isaiah whispered a thank you.

"For what?" Monica asked, staring up at the van's ceiling.

"Everything." Isaiah had said it so quietly it was almost inaudible, but Monica understood exactly what he had meant.

"You're welcome."

The sun rose warmly on the following June morning, marking the first time in Monica's life Katherine wasn't asleep in the room next door. It peeked over the top of the department store she and Isaiah had spent the night in front of, and by the time Monica woke up, it had risen high enough that it was almost completely visible over the endless rows of buildings and houses to the east.

Monica looked over at Isaiah, who was still fast asleep and climbed out of the van, stretching her arms and yawning. Her body was stiff from the hours spent lying on top of a single beach towel left over from the previous summer, crusty with salt and sand.

She pulled herself onto the hood of the van and watched as the sun rose higher.

The parking lot was empty, and, being dawn on a Sunday morning, the streets were silent. This was something

Monica was unaccustomed to. She fell asleep every night listening to cars hauling down the street adjacent to her house, watching their headlights light up her faded pink walls, and hearing planes fly overhead, wondering where they were coming from and where they were going.

    Who, she wondered, sat in the tight economy seats? What were their stories, she asked herself. She found it hard to imagine that real, full-sized people could fit into something so inanimate. She wanted to know each and every one of the people that sat on those planes, some feeling sick from the motion, some longing to get home to see their families, some dreading the impending business conferences they would have to sit through once the wheels touched the tarmac.

    She always loved it when the planes were forced to make another loop around before landing; it meant she got to inspect them again. The planes were so close to her house that she could clearly read the words written in large font on the side, which helped her imagine what the passenger's lives consisted of. Sometimes, she could even read the tail numbers but never desired to look up the flight plans online, which would have only taken a few seconds.

    She liked not knowing if her predictions were correct or not. She liked being able to picture the anonymous people sitting quietly as whoever she desired them to be. She imagined some coming from far away places she had never heard of.

    Monica had never been on a plane herself.

That morning, however, sitting on the hood of her twenty-year-old van, was completely silent, a silence Monica was almost uncomfortable by.

The blanket of stillness was ripped by the noise of one of the van's doors opening and then slamming shut.

Isaiah landed his bare feet on the pavement and surveyed the area, stretching his arms. He turned to look in the same direction as Monica's gaze.

"Oh, wow," he expressed quietly. He heaved himself onto the hood of the van beside Monica, displacing some of her weight. Isaiah was too infatuated by the picturesque sunrise to notice.

"I never really see the sunrise," he added once he settled.

"Really?" Monica asked, pulling her legs closer to her chest.

"No. I'm always asleep. I guess I never really thought it was super important. I mean, you're alive for so many of them, you kind of assume that they're all the same; you've seen it all. Last time I saw a sunrise I must have been like ten years old."

"You never really stop to think about how profound every moment is. Then one day you realize you don't have that many sunrises left. Instead of slowing down and appreciating the little things though, once people realize they're dying, they've been dying since the minute they were born, they speed up. They think they have so much more left to do, and then they overwork themselves to the point that they don't have the energy to marvel at the beauty of the world. *Wise* people say the little things are what make life worthwhile, but most people are so focused on the big picture, they never take the time to live." Monica continued to stare at the sky, but Isaiah turned to look at her.

"You're weird. Has anyone ever told you that?"

"Plenty of people have, but something's not true just because a lot of people say it is. Besides, I like being weird. It keeps it interesting." Isaiah laughed slightly, and Monica turned to look at him and smiled.

"We should probably get going," she added.

The Immigrant

Isaiah insisted that Monica leave him in the parking lot of the department store, and after much deliberation, Monica obliged.

When she looked at him in her rearview mirror one last time before turning onto the road, he was still watching the sunrise with a new sense of purpose and passion, a smile on his lips and a gleam in his eyes. Monica smiled to herself, hoping Isaiah's brother would eventually come to understand.

He wouldn't (at least not for many years). This was because it took Isaiah many years to work up the courage to punch his brother's number into his phone and explain that he had simply reached his breaking point and was afraid of what he thought was his only other option. His brother, through tears of his own (it relieved some of Isaiah's worries to hear his brother cry after years of silence), said he should have just told him how he had felt and that he would have supported Isaiah's decisions no matter what.

Although this did make Isaiah regret the impulsivity of his actions, he would not have traded in the life he got for anything.

A month after Monica left him alone in a parking lot to appreciate the beauty of a blue sky and a bright June morning, Isaiah shimmied his way across a dance floor and asked the prettiest woman he had ever seen to join him. She, with a smile, grabbed his hand and let him lead her into the crowd.

They spent the next two years having picnics in parks, watching movies into the early morning, and laughing hysterically at each other. This woman, named Caroline, encouraged Isaiah to express his emotions, desires, and needs in any way he felt necessary. He found a job working in human resources at a law firm and later asked Caroline to marry him; she gladly accepted. Isaiah finally worked up the courage to call his brother when he found out he was going to father a set of twins. Caroline and Isaiah chose to name their daughters Maria and Monica, and Isaiah's brother became their godfather.

After leaving Isaiah on his own to achieve all his goals in life, not within the time frame he had originally imagined but eventually, Monica merged back onto the highway. Unbeknownst to her, she had reached the halfway point of her journey to Miami.

Realizing she had not eaten anything since the afternoon prior, she pulled into a drive-thru line and ordered a cheeseburger. She knew this was not the most nutritious thing she could have gotten for breakfast, and her mother probably would have shot her a dirty look and told her if she kept eating like that she was going to get fat (as if that was the worst thing in the world that could happen to her).

Katherine seemed to have a minor obsession with Monica's weight but more so with her own. She would weigh herself three times a day, and when she was heavier at night, she would pull at her stomach and examine herself in the mirror, comparing her forty-year-old body to the ones of models half her age magazine editors and social media influencers told her she should look like.

Although Katherine knew her expectations were irrational, she couldn't help but give in to the pressure. She had tried her hardest to raise her only daughter in a supportive and understanding household but could not curb the standards she placed on herself.

She partly blamed her mother, who only made appearances in Katherine's life to tell her that she would never be good enough at anything.

Her mother had made weekly trips to the local drug store to buy platinum blond hair dye and whatever the newest weight loss supplement was throughout Katherine's childhood. Once her children grew up, she forced the same obsessions into them.

Katherine had never once seen her mother eat anything but a few crackers before dinner, where she would only eat a bite or two of the already limited quantity of food she served her family.

Katherine blamed her mother for her insecurities and couldn't afford the help she needed (even though she would have reverted to her old habits after only a day or two).

Monica had grown up watching her mother criticize herself but never understood her reasoning. Why, she wondered, would anyone be ashamed of the thing that gives them life, that has carried them for so long? She understood before her tenth birthday that many people felt the need to make themselves smaller, prettier, or ditzier to better fit society's standards; these standards were the only things they had ever been taught. They had watched rich and famous people who had personal trainers, chefs and home gyms and were told that was what the ideal person looked like. They

What If We Woke Up?

were told that it didn't matter how much they had accomplished, how many children they had given birth to or created, or how intelligent, kind, or successful they were; if they weren't a zero, they would never be good enough to be confident with something they did not have full control over.

    Monica, for some reason unbeknownst to Katherine, never fell victim to such thinking. She had eaten real food and not once, at least from Katherine's perspective, had she regretted it. She was glad her daughter had grown to understand beauty is a construct. This is what made Katherine the most frustrated; she was proud of her daughter for not being afraid to keep her body running.

    Monica couldn't afford to buy a traditional breakfast, so she settled on the cheeseburger. As she was pulling out of the line, peeling the wrapper off her meal, a man stepped in front of the van, requesting her to stop.

    Confused, Monica rolled down the window and addressed the man with a simple hello. He looked unwilling to get out of the way of the five thousand pound van.

    "Are you going south?" The man asked in an accent Monica could not pinpoint.

    Pausing for a moment to weigh her options, Monica added: "Yeah. You need a ride?"

    "Would you?" The man asked in a tone that told Monica she was not the first person he had stopped, but she was the first person that hadn't ignored him entirely. This encouraged Monica to confirm her original response.

"Yeah," she added. He praised her with his hands and walked around the van. Monica unlocked the passenger door, and he pulled himself in, sitting down and sighing.

"Thank you so much," he gushed. "Really, thank you. You have no idea how much this means."

"No problem," Monica responded, reading the desperation in his tone. "Where are you headed?"

"Well," he said. "My daughter is to turn fifteen at the end of the week, so I must go home to see her before her quinceanera."

"Oh, wow," Monica stated. "That's so exciting."

"Yes, very exciting. I just finished a week here."

"Doing what?"

"Well, for work, you understand."

"Sure," she said. "What do you do?"

"Building. We had to drive very far for this one, I live two hours away, you see, but my friend, he drove me this way, he got very sick and had to leave early. So now I have no one to drive me to see my daughter. This is why I must thank you."

"Oh, yeah. It's no big deal," Monica added.

"My daughter thanks you too," the man said as Monica smiled in return. "I could not miss such a big day for her."

"Of course not. What happens at a quinceanera?" Monica asked.

"Oh," said the man. "Well, it is similar to the sixteen you have."

"Oh, wow. So it's a big deal?"

What If We Woke Up?

"Yes, even bigger," he added. "I cannot believe it. It was not long ago that she was just my little girl. I cannot believe she is so old. I cannot believe it. Thank you so much for driving, I appreciate it."

"Don't worry about it. I was going this way anyway."

"I know they would be sad if I was not to be there. So thank you."

"What's your name?" Monica asked as she took the first bite of the burger.

"Luis," the man responded. "And you?"

"Monica."

"Monica: A very pretty name."

"Thank you," she added.

"I must apologize for my terrible English, as well. I have been told it is very bad."

"What?" Monica said, swallowing. "No. It's actually better than a lot of people I know."

"Is that true?" Luis questioned, a hint of pride in his voice.

"Yeah, totally," Monica responded. "A lot of people, people I just graduated with, they don't know the difference between there, their, and they're."

"I can't say I know either."

"Is English your first language?"

"No. It is not. I did not live here when I was young. I came here because life is very hard, you know. It still is. Even here."

"That's understandable though. If you already speak a language, that's one thing, but the fact that it's their first and they don't know how to properly communicate and write is a horrible reflection on the education system. Everyone I graduated high school with knows how to do the Macarena and the Cotton Eye Joe, but no one knows how to do taxes. No one knows how to apply for a job or raise a family. Why is it that the most important things in life are never taught by the people that are supposed to be doing exactly that?"

"I cannot tell you. My daughter brings home her work to do at home and asks me to help. I tell her I do not know how to do it. I do not know the things she is learning. All of the equations... they are just a bunch of letters. My daughter...she does not like math, she is not good at math; she wants to be a teacher for the little children. Why does she learn the big numbers?"

"Like, I get that it's teaching reasoning skills and how to learn and everything, but you would think there'd be a little bit more emphasis on the things that are essential to eke out an existence. At a certain point, some things need to be taught."

"I must agree with you. The reason I came here in the first place is for my children. My wife said she would not have our children not getting the right education. We knew they must be able to learn. It is much better than the other choice, but I can not say I am truly happy. My youngest son, he is six now, I do not know how I got this old-" They shared a quick laugh. "He was being yelled at by one of the teachers the week before this because he..." Luis stopped talking, making an expression that suggested he was attempting to remember something. "I cannot remember what it is called. It is when the letters are backward and upside down. Something like that"

"I don't know."

"He says he cannot read the letters. I can never remember what they call it. There are different letters in it?"

"Is it dyslexia maybe?"

"Yes," Luis added enthusiastically. "My wife always gets mad at me forgetting. I cannot say it, but that is what it is."

"Why was he getting yelled at?"

"Well, you see, the teacher thinks he is not telling the truth. He is making it up. He could not have it, it is not real, she says."

"Oh my god."

"That is what I said."

"That's horrible."

"Yes. It is. I do not know what I am going to do about it. Now he knows he is the only one in his class. Before he thought that was how everyone was. How do I tell him it is not?"

"I have no idea," Monica said. "If the teacher hadn't said anything, he might not have even realized."

"I don't believe he would."

Monica shook her head, her resentment for people that spoke before considering the implications of their words growing by the minute. Monica never minded listening to other people speak; in fact, she often enjoyed hearing other people's opinions. She believed everyone was entitled to their own until it offended someone else's existence.

"That's just frustrating."

"Yes. I come here so he can get a proper education, but what do I get? He gets made fun of. And my other daughter, she is the middle, she is fourteen. How many years do you have?"

"Eighteen."

"Oh goodness," Luis said. "You are much younger than I thought you to be."

"That's what everyone's told me," she responded with a laugh.

"You are not much older than my children."

"Yeah. I guess so."

"So my middle daughter, she had a girlfriend, you understand."

"Sure," Monica nodded.

"But her girlfriend moved away to another town, and now, in the autumn, my daughter will be going to the high school alone. I am worried for her."

"How come?"

"My wife wanted them to go to a school you must pay for, but the one she chose is very religious. They do not even allow the teaching of real science. My wife says it is the best education they can get, but I do not believe my daughter will be welcomed there, you understand."

Monica huffed in a disgruntled manner.

"Does your wife know that? Have you talked to her about it?"

"She says that education is the most important. If you are educated, she says to me every day, you will have nothing more to worry about. I do not think I agree completely with her, but she is always right in my house. I am just afraid that these children will be even more mean to her than the ones at the last school."

Monica was growing increasingly frustrated. She herself had had her share of experiences with bullies and the likes over the course of her eighteen years of life. She heard the whispers people talked with when she walked by. These immature children, who would never outgrow their inane practices, talked just loudly enough they were sure Monica could hear them.

Monica had lived a fairly nonexistent existence for all twelve of her years in school. She would wake up every morning, eat two pieces toast with butter (Katherine had requested she stop eating a bagel with peanut butter and an apple on the side because "well, you know sweetheart, that's not gonna be good for you"), sit in traffic for ten minutes, attend school, plop herself on her bed, and finish her homework. After dinner, she would sit down in front of the television at seven-thirty and test her knowledge with the help of Alex Trebek.

To fill her long, boring days, she would often play games to entertain herself. Once, she kept track of how many words she said each day. After completing the experiment, she found she uttered significantly less than the average person. She spoke only when prompted, and only when the prompting was regarding a topic that interested her.

This essentially enabled Monica Lewis to live in the shadows of her Massachusetts high school. Although she did have a few acquaintances, she spent most of her days in silence. She didn't bother anyone else, and, for the most part, other people paid no mind to her either. This was an existence Monica was content living.

However, some days were harder than others. Sometimes she would convince herself that everyone she passed was whispering about her. Although she was generally confident in herself, she sometimes couldn't help letting her inner insecurities cause her imagination to run wild.

Other times, the whispers were really about her. Attention hungry people would taunt her (and countless others) across the hallways to fit in with the crowd. Monica would come to realize that these wannabe-tormentors were generally well-meaning and kind people individually, but when put into a group, they became toxic. They each lost themselves in the quest to fit in with the crowd, which was made up of people trying to do the same thing. Anonymity turned decent people into oppressors.

These kids were conditioned to believe the only way to get noticed was to be the loudest one in the crowd of unnamed faces. They jumped, screamed, kicked, and fought to claim their place at the top of the social ladder. Once they got there, they became feared.

Monica, at a young age, came to realize that this never-ending search for the top did not end with a diploma. Katherine had oftentimes come home complaining of a coworker, and Monica concluded that she would have to put up with people who had learned material and social success equates to happiness, which directly opposed Monica's own beliefs, for the rest of her life. She resented this fact.

"Do you think your daughter knows?" Monica asked.

"She knows what?"

"Why she might not be welcomed?"

"I think she does know, but she is unsure why. You see, that is the only thing she has ever known, you understand. She does not think that she is...how you say...different. She does not know how much some people hate."

"It's horrible. I'm so sorry that's the world we live in."

"Yes. I am sure she will be fine. She will learn to dance."

"That might just be public schools (probably not though)."

"We will see in the autumn."

"Yeah."

"Can I ask a question of you?" Luis asked.

"Go for it," Monica responded.

"How does one raise a child that is such as you?" Monica laughed at this. She had never really put much thought into how her mother's parenting style led her to become the person she was. She did understand how much of an impact a person's environment has on their outcome. However, she believed that in addition to being a product of genetics and surroundings, people were also products of their imaginations.

"I think," Luis continued. "You seem much older than, what did you say, eighteen?"

"Yeah. People have always told me that, but I think you'd be surprised. Yeah, we don't have as many experiences, but we know more than you might think we do. We're young and naive, but that doesn't mean we're completely incompetent. I think the further you get from your own teenage years, the more you forget about your experience. Parents forget how old they felt when they were our age, even though we might not really be. Age is just a number. I mean, I was thinking about this the other day...I remember when I was in fifth grade the things we used to gossip about on the bus and the playground...our parents and teachers would have been horrified to realize how much of the world we understood. Even now, I look at young kids, and I think to myself, *wow, you know a whole lot more than everyone thinks you do.* That's what scares me most about aging, you know. You forget what it was like; you can no longer relate to anyone younger than you. Maybe we haven't fully matured, but we're not idiots."

"Oh," Luis stated.

"People don't realize how much the world has changed either. Some parents think that because things worked for them when they were our age, it's gonna work for us too. There's a whole different culture. A lot of teenagers are struggling. A lot of teenagers don't know who they are or what they want to be. At the same time though, there's a connection we have as a generation. We all know the world right now is a difficult place to grow up in, and everyone jokes about death and dying, and we're all cool with it. Our generation is weird. We're too scared to order our own ice cream, but we'll stand up for what we believe is right. We connect over our shared understanding of the darkness of the world, and other generations just don't understand that. There's a whole subculture. I am young; I'll be the first to admit it, but at the same time, I know a lot more about the world than other people think I do. I'm capable of things you might not expect."

"This makes me very nervous to think about what my oldest daughter knows." Monica laughed as Luis's face became deeply concerned.

"Sorry about that," Monica added, her laughs subsiding.

"This is okay. I was thinking it might be time to give her a talk, but I am guessing she already knows, by what you said." Monica laughed.

She took the last bite of her cheeseburger before crumpling up the wrapper and throwing it into the back of the van, which had become her trash can. She was surprised by how much waste a single person could generate even just over the course of a few hours. She had always noticed that whenever she and her mother drove to the mountains of New Hampshire, the mansions of Rhode Island, or the beaches of Maine, she would walk back into her house afterward with an ungodly amount of trash. She would also have an empty coffee cup, wrappers, socks, a book, and a pair of earbuds.

Those earbuds only worked when she configured the wires in a certain position, but she continued to use them to drown out her mother's awkward and oppressing silence.

Katherine often made fun of Monica's taste in music, which did not consist of a certain genre or artist but rather simply of songs Monica enjoyed listening to.

Katherine's disdain for many of Monica's favorites led her to a certain level of secrecy. To avoid disappointing her mother, Monica oftentimes kept her opinions to herself. She preferred to read books, watch movies, listen to songs, and consume all forms of art without her mother's negative input. Katherine enjoyed very specific genres, actors, and writers. All else, Katherine believed, was to be looked down upon in scorn.

This also held true for Katherine's political beliefs. She automatically agreed with whatever the candidate belonging to her party said, never stopping to consider the ways in which she would have approached the situation. She refused to even listen to the other party's view, thinking everything they said was purely fiction and propaganda.

This was something Monica did not understand at all. She thought the reason the highest forms of government are so filled with corruption, greed, and gridlock is that politicians, voters, and donors refuse to break party lines to stand up for what would be best for the people. Government officials tag along with their party simply because they do not want to become the outlier.

True political greatness, Monica thought, could only be achieved when politicians worked for the people instead of working solely to advance the agenda of their party.

"I think you should," Monica said. "Just knowing that you're there to support her no matter what is more important than anything else. If you talk to her now, she won't be as afraid to come to you later on about the big things. You're setting a precedent. Either way, she's probably gonna end up in that situation, even though that probably does scare you, so by showing her that it is all right, she's gonna be more open and probably a lot smarter as well. I wish I had gotten that, even though it would have been awkward at the moment. Besides, it won't be her first time hearing about it, even if she does go to a conservative school."

"You think I should say it?"

"I know you should," Monica finished.

"I think that I am going to then," Luis added with a flourish of his head.

"Good. I'm sure she'll be grateful."

The Woman

Monica got off the highway to drop Luis off at his house, which was only a mile or two out of her way. They stopped at a well-kept suburban home with a perfectly manicured lawn and a freshly painted white picket fence, and she said a final goodbye to Luis, hoping he and his family would live their versions of happily ever after. There were two sprinklers watering the lawn, and the man across the street was pushing a mower over his own. This, thought Monica, was the embodiment of the American dream.

The neighborhood was composed of spacious, tidy homes with generous front lawns. Visitors were welcomed by the sounds of dogs barking, kids playing, and ice cream trucks driving. This was a life Monica would have been content living.

She could picture herself settling comfortably inside one of these homes surrounded by friends and family. She would host cocktail parties for her neighbors, allowing her to catch up on the latest local scandals. She would hear about job transfers, homework, and baseball games.

For a moment, Monica questioned her dream. She understood clearly that she had not yet discovered her passion and purpose in life. She became slightly jealous of Tessa, who wanted to be a writer, James, who wanted to be accepted, Isaiah, who wanted a family of his own, Luis, who wanted prosperity for his kids, and even Katherine, who wanted to one-up Barbra at everything. What, she wondered, did she want?

Only a few days prior, she had wanted nothing more than to evade the norm. With the realization that she had known only that she wanted to leave the street she grew up on, she was left without something to hold onto.

It would have been much easier for her to simply accept the standard American life. She could have attended college, graduated, gotten a job, and visited her mother on weekends. She could have settled for an acceptable Massachusetts man and raised a family of her own. She could have retired and lived the rest of her days as a snowbird. Maybe she made the move to the south prematurely, she thought momentarily.

Why, she wondered, could she not accept that she was not special? She understood that everyone wanted to do something interesting and unique with their own life. Yet, most of them eventually conformed and were, at the end, satisfied with the decisions they had made. Had she simply been too quick to follow her instincts? Would those thoughts have diminished if she had accepted the standard?

This was the first time in a while that Monica doubted her intuition. She had always thought she was strong enough to live the life that others had not expected for her, but was she simply trying too hard to be the outlier?

She had no special talent. She could not sing, she could not dance, she could not paint, she could not write. She was not an exceptional student. She was simply herself. This caused her, as she pulled away from Luis's home, him waving goodbye to her, to question what her purpose really was.

She was well aware of the fact that she only had one life and did not want to waste it on something boring and dull, but she had no real, concrete goals. What she wanted one day, she might not want the next.

She knew, however, she was not an anomaly. In the few conversations she had had with her peers, she had concluded that not a single teenager truly knew what they wanted the entirety of their life to look like, but they were expected to.

Teachers and college admissions officers and parents all put pressure on these kids to finalize their lives after only eighteen years of testing the waters (even though they tested those waters wearing goggles, flippers, a gallon and a half of sunblock, and water wings).

The vast majority of these swimmers had no idea what they wanted to be when they grew up, and even though the well-meaning adults in their lives didn't know what they wanted for themselves either, they continuously put pressure on their young, untrained kids to figure out who they were.

It was almost the expectation that graduating seniors had every second of every decade of their lives written down in black and white, even though they, in reality, could not even decide which restaurant to go to for dinner after receiving their diploma.

Parents and teachers also expected greatness from every one of these wide-eyed students. They expected a secondary education, a successful job, enough money to make regular weekend trips to the lake house, and a happy, healthy family, when in reality, most of them would end up falling asleep in lecture halls, struggling to cook edible food, and breaking up and making up on the daily.

These children's parents expected both material and emotional success, but this pressure inhibited both of those things.

Although Katherine only desired for Monica to be more successful than Barbra's son, Monica understood that most kids received that same kind of expectation in all sectors of life.

Monica knew only that she wanted to do something interesting. She had not set out to do something extraordinary but feared that in living the life she had originally wanted, she would never reach her full potential, the extent of which she did not yet understand. Maybe, she thought, she would never be satisfied, and she would never stop wishing for something more.

She continued to ponder her doubts and feelings of inadequacy as she pulled into another rest stop, hoping that in the five minutes she would spend away from her van her emotions would stabilize.

Her stream of thought was momentarily interrupted when a woman walked out of the bathroom, wiping her hands on the front of her sleeveless black shirt, and looked in Monica's direction.

By this point, Monica was versed in the appearance of a hitchhiker, and the woman did not even need to open her mouth before Monica once again offered her extra seat.

She hoped this woman would offer a distraction from her nagging insecurities.

The two women, Monica and Anne, as it turned out the woman was named, continued down the road together. Monica wanted to know where Anne was from and where she was going.

"Well," Anne started with a chuckle. "At the moment, I'm just kind of seeing where the wind takes me. I planned to go on a road trip with my boyfriend, but he decided some girl he met at some club was better than I was, so, naturally, because I already took the time off, I figured I'd do it by myself. Can I give you a piece of advice?"

"Sure." Anne shifted in her chair, flopping around to face Monica. She crossed her legs over each other.

"Wait. She?"

"What?" Monica responded.

"Do you go by she and her?"

"Oh, yeah. You?"

"Yeah. Okay. You don't need a guy. Yeah, sometimes it's nice, but you know what: you're just as strong on your own. I think my ex just thought I was too strong for him."

"That's a good problem to have," Monica added with a laugh.

"It really is. I'd just like to apologize, hon. I really would."

"For what?" Monica asked, a hint of apprehension in her voice.

"It's rough out there. People tell you you have to look a certain way, you have to feel a certain way, you have to act a certain way. You don't. Who said that? Nobody said that; it's just something we all for whatever reason believe.

What If We Woke Up?

It's ridiculous. You know what makes me mad?" Monica, at that moment, realized she likely would not be given many chances to speak; she was entirely willing to embrace this.

"I hate it when people associate such a negative connotation with feminist. Like, I'm afraid to even use that word because people get so fired up, and I'm sure you already know that never ends well. How old are you?"

"Eighteen."

"I just think it shouldn't be that hard to even the playing field. Enough of favoring one gender. Enough of favoring one skin tone or economic class or background or sexuality. Why can't we all just be treated fairly? That doesn't mean not seeing differences. That means respecting differences, respecting history, understanding everyone's backgrounds, and supporting them in living their own lives. None of us are the same, and we might never understand what someone else has gone through, so we all just need to respect each other's existence. It fires me up, you know. Everyone says America is the land of the free, but with such bias against certain groups of people, I'm not too sure it is. If you're not a straight, cis, white dude with a decent inheritance, you automatically lose respect in every social setting, and that's ridiculous. You're looked at like you're weaker when in reality, you're just as capable as anyone else. The only way to actually become the 'greatest country in the world,' whatever that means, is to listen to all voices and ideas equally, no matter how out of the box or nontraditional they are. That's the only way we'll ever get anything done. If we continue to work in the same way we have been we'll never get anywhere. We can't be such traditionalists. We have to be willing to let go of the past. Now, I'm not saying that we need to completely change or forget everything or something like that; I'm just saying that we can't be afraid of the future. We can't be so afraid to right our ancestor's wrongs. We have to let every voice be heard, and that's not something that's happening right now. It's sad. It really is."

"Wow," Monica asserted, unsure of what else she could add to the conversation. She figured Anne would continue on her own without much input from Monica; she would.

"Yeah, wow is right. It makes me mad. The world would be a whole lot nicer of a place if we all treated everyone with the respect they deserve."

"I think I have to agree with you."

"Just don't ever let anyone tell you that you're not as good as someone else. You know what else makes me mad?"

"Sounds like a lot of things." Anne laughed.

"You're not wrong." Anne began. "Now, I think the real problem is that a lot of guys think that we're looking to take over, not just make things equal, you know. They feel almost threatened by us. They've had all the power for so long that they're afraid to grasp the fact that we're just as capable as they are. We just want to be treated as equals. Not better, not worse: equal. Some people think that if we're successful, they should be able to hit us. That's not even what we're talking about, and that just says a lot about their unchecked aggression, if that's their first thought. We just want to be paid equally for the same amount of work. We want the same opportunities. We want the same respect. We don't need to be better; we just need to be equal. We want to be listened to."

"I agree."

"Look back a hundred years ago. Women couldn't vote. Women didn't have any rights in marriage. They had the social status of a child. Their only job was to raise the next generation of men, who in turn would go on to treat their wives like servants. It shocks me that they thought it was okay, you know. Their mothers raised them. They were successful because of their mother's influence, but then they grew up to look down on women as a whole. All this means is that we have to put in the work now so our daughters can get the respect we were never given."

"I've always been of the belief that instead of teaching our daughters to arm themselves, we should teach our sons to keep their hands to themselves. We should also be teaching them that this goes both ways. Men can also become victims of abuse and manipulation. Just because the numbers suggest that women are more often targeted doesn't mean that men aren't at all. Honestly, I think if there wasn't such a stigma for men to talk about their experiences, those numbers would be a whole lot higher. When the whole concept of toxic masculinity is addressed and there is no longer the expectation for men to be emotionless and strong at all times, everyone will benefit.

"I'm not a very physically imposing person. I'm not super loud or scary. I've been conditioned to always be on the lookout. Every person I pass makes me nervous. I think every car that goes by is gonna stop and scoop me up. I think everybody I walk by is gonna hurt me. I hold my keys as a weapon. Sometimes I think I should cover up a little bit more just so people don't blame me and say I was asking for it, even though it would have happened no matter what I was wearing. I don't feel safe walking across a parking lot by myself. It should be almost unfathomable to believe that's the reality in twenty-first-century America. School taught me more about the danger of showing my shoulders than about paying taxes." Anne shook her head, Monica's words making her even more passionate.

"A couple of months ago I went for a jog on a trail," she began. "A lot of families walk on it, but it was super hot out. I had on shorts and a t-shirt, right, and I was starting to overheat a little bit, so I took my shirt off to cool down. Now I'm not by any means saying I have the perfect body or anything, and that's fine with me. I really like ice cream. That's fine with me. I never even really think about how I look, and that's something I am thankful for. Anyways, I was just jogging down the trail. I was sweating pretty badly. I think I had forgotten to put on deodorant. My hair was soaked with sweat and sticking to my face. My thighs were chafing. I was wheezing. Still, every single guy that I passed *studied* me as I slogged down the trail. I even turned around once and one of them was still watching me. These guys were walking with their wives. They were holding hands with their children. One of them was even carrying his daughter on his shoulders. I just want to live in a world where I can run down the street without everyone gawking at me like they've never seen a bare stomach before. I want to live in a world where people look at me and respect that

I'm getting some exercise instead of fantasizing. I want to be taken seriously instead of being laughed at for trying to get what I want. If I know what I want, I'm aggressive, I'm a diva; I'm not just someone voicing their opinion. If I were to tell someone what it was actually like, I wouldn't be believed. They'd tell me I'm making it up; I can't take a joke. They'd tell me I'm being dramatic; I'm overreacting. I've been called power-hungry time and time again because I know what I want and what it'll take to get there. When a man knows what he wants, he's driven, he's a hustler."

"This isn't necessarily related, but I just remembered it."

"I'm all ears," Anne said passionately.

"When I was younger, my mom took me out to get ice cream one day during the summer. My favorite flavor has always been strawberry, so, naturally, I knew that's what I wanted. So we got to the front of the line, and the lady asked me what I wanted, and immediately I said strawberry. She goes 'oh, wow, you know what you want' in an almost condescending tone. I know that's not really a big deal, but it's always stuck with me: the fact that it's the expectation that I wouldn't know what I wanted for whatever reason when in reality everyone has a favorite flavor of ice cream, you know. Comments like that are the reason I'm so afraid to speak up."

"We're told things like that our whole lives. You shouldn't know what you want. Then when we say 'I don't know' we're told we're difficult to deal with, when in reality, it's a defense mechanism to protect ourselves from the inevitable ridicule. Every time I walk through the supermarket, there's some old guy that makes some derogatory comment. One tells me I shouldn't be wearing shorts because I'm tempting him, or I'm asking for it. One says I should smile. What do I have to smile about? In fact, in telling me that, you're giving me a reason not to smile. When I order dessert after dinner, I'm told I should lay off the calories, but if I did, they'd tell me to eat a cheeseburger. I go home for the holidays and my uncle's asking me why I don't have a boyfriend. The other uncle's telling me I should never even think about a guy like that. My grandfather's yelling about how he wants to be a great grandfather. My cousin's asking me about my activity, which I won't answer because his response is going to be to tell me I'm either a whore or a bore. My mother's telling me I shouldn't be having a second slice of pumpkin pie. My brother's telling me I'm being too emotional. My other cousin's telling me I need to cook and clean. My step brother's telling me I should learn how to change a tire, but his mother's telling me that I shouldn't get my hands dirty. My aunt and uncle are off somewhere screaming at each other and threatening to get divorced while their son is off in the other room crying about it. All the while I'm just trying to enjoy the 'most wonderful time of the year.'"

"We've been told our whole lives that men are superior at everything except for controlling their anger, and that's the expectation," Monica said.

"You know, I'm really glad you agree with me. Most times when I start to tell someone this, they tell me I'm being overdramatic."

"That only adds validity to your argument."

"Exactly," Anne said, her arms flailing wildly in enthusiastic passion. "That's literally what I've been saying. The world is gonna be a better place because people like you (and me, but that's beside the point) are in it. The only way we're gonna get the future we so desperately need is by continuing to fight for just basic equalities for all genders, sexualities, races, and classes. I think our job is to make things a little bit easier and fairer for the next generation. If we can ensure that our kids and grandkids inherit a better world than we have now, we've done our job. We have to add to the legacy that is the American tradition, even though it may be completely messed up right now. If people were a little more understanding of each other, we'd get there a whole lot faster."

The Teenager

By the time Monica left Anne at the next rest stop they passed, the sun was beginning to set. They had spent upwards of two hours discussing all sectors of the American experience before parting ways.

Monica surveyed her surroundings before trying to sneak across the parking lot, ensuring she was not being watched. She wanted, for only a few miles, to be truly alone.

This would be too much to ask, for sometimes her imagination truly would run wild.

A girl holding an iced coffee, who did not look much older than Monica herself, stepped out of the bathroom, sighing with relief at the sight of someone who appeared trustworthy. She rushed over to Monica, who was slightly annoyed by the prospect of another companion. She had never had this much social contact in her eighteen years of life and was growing tired.

"Hey," the girl started when she first approached Monica, who smiled back at her softly. "You goin' south?" She finished.

Monica nodded and added a soft "yes."

"Any chance you could give me a ride?"

"Sure," Monica said with a light sigh.

"Thanks so much, bro. Seriously. My dad would have killed me if I told him some sus guy drove me." Monica laughed as this girl surveyed the parking lot.

"Why can't your dad drive you?" The girl simply shrugged her shoulders in response, slurping on her metal straw.

The girl sat down in the passenger seat of Monica's van as Monica started the engine once again.

They began traveling down the highway at a comfortable eighty miles an hour.

"What's your name?" Monica asked, finally breaking the silence. Neither of them, however, had seemed uncomfortable.

"Elizabeth," the girl responded. "But you can call me whatever." Monica laughed at this.

"Where are you going?"

"Well, I'm tryna get to my dad's house for the weekend. Just cause like...I have to. Legally, you know. Not that I want to, but it's fine, I guess."

"That's annoying."

"Facts."

"Makes me kind of glad I can't see my dad, honestly."

"Oop. Sis." Elizabeth covered her mouth with her fist. Monica laughed and looked over at Elizabeth, who was staring at the dashboard, her eyes opened widely.

"It's all good."

"I guess you are lucky then." Monica laughed lightly.

"How old are you?" was the next question Monica asked.

"Sixteen," Elizabeth answered, shifting in the seat.

"That's fun."

"Is it? Is it really?" Elizabeth looked back at Monica.

"Sure. Why wouldn't it be?" Monica asked.

"Well, I don't know about you, but I don't really wanna live, so. What's the point at this point, yanno."

"You're serious?"

"Yeah."

"Really?"

"You're telling me you actually have an interest in living?"

"I don't know."

"Monica you said your name was?"

"Yeah."

"Well, you're the first person my age I've ever met that's said that."

"What does that say about society?"

"Everyone knows the world's burning," Elizabeth said, focusing her attention on the potholes dotting the road. "Nobody has a clue how to actually live. We're all just faking it till we make it. The economy makes it almost impossible to thrive, you know. Politicians are incompetent. We're all depressed." Elizabeth looked over at Monica. "You really haven't thought about it?"

"I mean, not really."

"Bro, you have to have thought about it."

"I guess."

"How would you do it?"

"Woah."

"I'll tell you how I'd do it."

"I don't think I want to know." Monica's tone became more concerned.

"I'm just joking, bro. Chill. I'd never actually. Well, not yet. I still have some hope for... yeah I don't even know anymore, but I couldn't do that to my family. That's not fair. So now I kinda have to live, and like, I'm not really here for it. It's unfair to think one day I was just born, and now here we are: forced to live. Animals are born and like literally five minutes later they got everything figured out. They're just vibin'. How is that fair? Tell me. How is that fair?"

"I don't know," Monica added. She was considerably taken aback by Elizabeth's rhetoric, but this was not the first time she had heard such a pattern of thinking.

Six months into Monica's sophomore year of high school, her lab partner stole his father's gun and disappeared into the night. His body was found three days later half-submerged in a creek that trickled into the town's water supply.

On the first day of school, the teacher had asked her students to get into the pairs they would sit in for the rest of the year. Monica and this boy, Travis, were the only two individuals without the popularity or the social skills to find a partner on their own. While the rest of the class walked around, arguing over who was going to be partners with the socialites of the school, Monica and Travis remained seated, swiveling their heads around the classroom, hoping they would catch the gaze of someone who pitied them enough to offer their partnership. No one was willing to sacrifice their social acceptance by associating with the low life of the class.

The teacher, after everyone else was sitting comfortably beside their *friends*, realized that Travis and Monica were still single. She, after expressing her discontent with their unwillingness to carry out the "simplest of tasks; it's not rocket science to find a partner," forced them to parade to the front of the classroom and sit down at the pair of desks closest to her so she could "keep an eye" on them. She didn't "want any funny business."

Monica and Travis spent the first half of the year awkwardly agreeing with wrong answers to avoid confrontation (at only fifteen, Monica had not yet worked up the courage to stand up for herself) until one day Travis didn't show.

The teacher suggested that if Monica had been a bit nicer to her partner, "this foolishness never would have happened."

"I'm just straight up not having a good time at this point," Elizabeth added. "It's not even just that though. We're all expected to have our lives figured out. I don't know what I wanna do. Bro, I don't wanna do anything. I don't wanna get out of bed in the morning, nevermind actually be productive. I don't wanna go to school. I don't wanna have to deal with other people. I don't even wanna sit down and watch a movie or something cause I feel like I should be doing something else."

"I get that."

"See, you know what I mean."

"I suppose," Monica said, her voice inflecting with the last syllable.

"Like, what's the point? We're all gonna die one day and none of it's gonna matter. My existence is completely irrelevant, and like, we're all totally aware of that fact, which is weird. So why can't I just do whatever I feel like, right? At the end of the day, people are all just sayin' that happiness is the most important thing, so why should I even wanna do things that don't make me happy?"

"I mean, I can see what you're saying."

"The only issue is that nothing makes me happy, so. Serotonin, amirite?" Monica let out a startled laugh and immediately covered her mouth.

"I'm so sorry," she said. "I just didn't expect you to say that."

"I mean, all signs were pointing in that direction, but, whatever, bro. Whatever floats your boat." Elizabeth turned her attention out the window. "I just don't wanna be average."

"That's what I've been saying," Monica responded, putting emphasis on each word.

"Like I'ma try to do things that make me feel at least decent, but like, I don't think I'll ever be good enough, you know. I know I'm not the prettiest person ever. I'm not the most popular. I'm not the funniest, the nicest, or the most athletic. I don't have any special talents. There's nothing that separates me from everyone else. I'll never be number one at anything." Monica sighed, relating to every word Elizabeth was saying.

"I know most people are average, and I don't think I'm special or anything like that, but there's so much pressure just to excel at everything. Bro, just a couple of weeks ago, I was making lunch and instead of putting the actual sandwich in my bag, I packed the knife I used to spread the peanut butter. I just licked it off and called it a day. I smashed my head off the cabinet door when I was leaving this morning. Lived in the same house my whole life. That cabinet has always been there. I was in Spanish class last week asking someone to pick something up and got sent to the principal's office for whatever reason. My boyfriend broke up with me last week because, I kid you not, his Ouija board told him to," Elizabeth finished, turning to look at Monica.

Monica once again tried to hold back her laughter.

"You can laugh at that one. That's all good." They shared a heartfelt laugh in response.

"Like my entire life at this point is made up of just doing stupid things. Not like the stupid things Hollywood says we should be doing though, you know."

"Oh, for sure," Monica added.

"Like, tbh, I've spent the last three years locked in my bedroom watching tv shows and eating ice cream from the carton. I'm not out every night, you know."

"I think that only lends itself to a feeling of inadequacy. When for as long as you can remember you've been told that these years are the best of your life, you've spent your days counting down to them. Now you're here, and it's not everything it's built up to be."

"Most of us are just tryin' not to cry in the middle of class, nevermind the club."

"The number of times I've witnessed that honestly would surprise people that have separated themselves so much from their youth. The fact that students hope that horrible things happen just so they don't have to go to school for a day or two says *a lot* about the education system as it is. I think we're living a completely different experience than our parents and grandparents. We all have total access to everything you could ever need to know, and that makes us almost hyper-aware and sensitive of our insecurities because the prototype of an American or a teenager has been shoved down our throats our whole lives."

"My grandmother keeps telling me like, oh 'I'm so proud of you' and all that kind of stuff, but in reality, I think it's just because she like doesn't have any model to compare me to, you know."

"I completely agree."

"Some people just don't understand that we're all struggling to wake up in the morning and function because we see how horrible the world is."

"The fact that we're all aware of what's going on in the world, and we could so easily choose to listen to one-sided, biased media outlets instead of looking for the truth has only made it harder to live. We understand the difficulties of life because we're living it."

"The people that write teenagers in movies or tv shows or books or whatever, they all think we're too naive and dumb to understand what the real world is. They think because it took them however many years to find out the truth, it's gonna take us just as long."

"When in reality that's the farthest thing from the truth. I honestly feel bad for people younger than us that have been exposed to these ridiculous expectations for literally their whole lives. They never really got an innocent childhood," Monica said. "We're told over and over again that the American experience is greatness, and we always have to be number one and all that kind of stuff, when in reality everything that *is* American culture is completely inhibiting and stunting our personal growth. The media, our families, technology, and a thousand other things are setting entirely unrealistic expectations."

"I gotta agree. Every adult is like 'these are the best years of your life. You should enjoy them,' and not that I wanna like do all the things we've been told teenagers do, but if I did they'd be like 'oh, don't do that. You can't drink and smoke and hit it and sneak out every night.' I just don't understand. Whatever we do isn't right, but whatever we don't do isn't right either. How does that make sense? Tell me."

"I don't know," Monica responded.

"Like, all I'm tryna do is get through the day so I'm a little bit closer to death. That's all I want."

"That's a terrifying reality."

"Like, I'm just doin' the best I can, and I get that's what everyone else is doin' too. My mom always says like 'oh, I don't know what I wanna do when *I* grow up' but then expects me to. I never said I was the perfect kid. I know I got my flaws, everyone does, right?"

"Definitely," added Monica passionately.

"I don't get why we're told to be things that just don't make sense. Make it make sense."

"We're all expected to be the embodiment of perfection when in reality that's just not possible for anyone to be. When I was younger, I was always the kid that got 'pleasure to have in class' written on my report card, but I only acted that way because I was so afraid of being reprimanded, punished, or called out. Parents and teachers don't want real children, they want obedient children. They want robots. They want children that are so afraid to express themselves because they don't believe they will be accepted when their completely normal flaws are brought into the limelight. Our worth is based solely on how willing we are to conform and listen, and because I obliged as a child, I'm now completely unequipped to deal with the *real world*. I have no idea how to stand up for myself, argue my point, or even how to engage in simple, necessary conversations."

"Remember when I asked you how you'd kill yourself, and you seemed surprised that I'd like even ask that?"

"As in like five minutes ago?"

"Yeah."

"Is that related?"

"You're the problem," Elizabeth stated bluntly.

"What?" Monica asked.

"You're the problem. Not you specifically, but."

"I don't know what that means."

"The fact that people are so unwilling to address the fact that that type of thinking exists literally everywhere you go makes it even harder to feel better. Like, the fact that we get almost ridiculed for not being okay makes it a thousand times worse. Instead of saying 'oh, never talk about that, that's a horrible thing to say,' maybe we should like offer a hand or something. That way when it eventually does happen you don't have to feel guilty. 'Hey, at least I tried to help.' But no, that's not what happens. We've been told our whole lives that the worst thing you could be is not okay, and I'm not talking about like a broken bone or cough or anything, I'm talking about everything we've been told makes us less of a person. A lot of people don't believe me because I haven't like lived through a warzone or anything like that. Everyone in my family says 'oh, that's such a horrible thing to say,' but when I work up the guts to go through with it, they'll be upset. They'll look down at me. They'll think 'oh, how could you put us through this mourning?' Maybe, grandma, if you hadn't kept drilling that it was unacceptable to look for any help into me, this wouldn't have happened.

"They don't get it, and I don't understand that. We're not living in an era where we have to stay quiet. If we have a voice, we're gonna use it, right? I think so. I'm not okay. I really am not, but unlike my ancestors, I refuse to be silenced. I refuse to pretend that everything's fine. If I'm at some stupid party and someone asks me how I am, I'ma tell them the truth, and when they can't handle it, I'ma tell them to grow up. I spend every night wondering what my future's gonna look like. Like, what happens if I don't pick the right career? What happens if I don't like my job? What happens if after I graduate, I realize I hate everything about the field? Everyone says you should do things that excite you, but honestly, the only thing that makes me excited is the end. You got me?"

"I don't-"

"Well, you what, bro? This is the world we live in. The people that are supposed to be leading us are stuck in the past. They think the privileged lives they've lived make them and everything they say more valid than someone who's lived a normal life. They're trying so hard to keep us out of the future, but you know what? People like me...we're not having it. If some old lady in the store asks me how I'm doing, you best believe I'm telling her I very well might go drive off a bridge. I'm not pretending to be okay anymore. I'm not pretending that I don't worry about every mistake I've ever made and every mistake I will ever make. I'm not pretending that the future that I don't even wanna live doesn't terrify me. What if I disappoint everyone? Is that gonna be the last straw? How do I know that it won't get better? How do I know that people who are willing to listen won't come into power and make life a little bit easier for everyone? How do I know when? How do I know that I will never wake up feeling excited? I have a whole life to live, and I know the impact taking myself out would have on other people, not because they really would have been willing to make things right, but because they know, even if they were given a second chance, they wouldn't have been able to bring themselves to talk to me, to offer me a hand.

"How do I know that'll I'll ever be enough? How do I know that I'll ever laugh again? One day, your mother picked you up for the last time. One day you skipped for the last time. One day you changed your doll's clothes for the last time. How do I know I haven't already experienced joy for the last time? One day your innocent view of the world ended. We aren't disillusioned because we never fell for it in the first place. One day, when I was in elementary school, I turned on the tv and saw kids my age get killed in a school shooting. One day, I turned on the tv and saw a man get murdered because he 'looked suspicious' but mostly because he was a little darker than everyone else in the neighborhood. I'm sixteen, and I can not tell you how many times I've turned on the television and been heartbroken. I don't even notice it anymore. This is the world we live in. This is the world we grew up in. This is the only world we've ever known. My most vivid childhood memories don't involve ice cream and puppies and swimming pools, they involve mass shootings and terrorist attacks. So when older people who grew up believing that the world is a decent place made of good people don't understand my desire for death, I guess I can kind of get it."

"I-" Monica started.

"I just don't get why you don't see it."

"I don't know," Monica said.

"Explain it to me. You know how bad it is. So tell me why you're fine with it."

"I don't believe I'm fine with the world we live in," Monica began. "I do understand the injustices, and I do at some points feel like it will never get better, but you know what?"

"Go off."

"This isn't the end. Just look at how far you've come. If you had already done it, you wouldn't be here right now. Your family's life would have been completely upheaved. There will be someone that stands up for other people, and you know what? They might not be here tomorrow, but eventually, the world is gonna look a lot different. Just the fact that you're talking about how much more accepting we are as a generation than others shows that the world can change for the better. I think our job is to make things a little bit easier for all other generations that follow us. Yeah, maybe right now isn't the best time to be alive, but neither was a hundred years ago, a thousand years ago. You don't know how much your own life could improve. Maybe one day you will find something or someone that makes you happy. Maybe you will find a passion, and even if it doesn't make you any money, as long as you like it, it'll be worth it. Maybe you'll enjoy collecting cacti. Maybe you'll find out you're a good cook or baker. Maybe you'll find a passion for reading books or binging tv shows. Maybe you'll find out you're a talented magician or you like playing the harmonica. Maybe you'll find joy in making candles or painting your fingernails or staging photoshoots. No matter what though, the fact that you're pulling yourself out of bed in the morning despite the dumpster fire raging around you is an accomplishment in and of itself."

"I guess so," Elizabeth said.

"You just have to promise me something."

"Okay."

"You won't date any more guys that are into Ouija boards."

The Homeless Man

Monica did eventually get the solitude she had longed for when, after stopping to go to the bathroom and relax for a moment (so much driving had made Monica extremely tired), Elizabeth told her that her father would be willing to pick her up from the rest stop. Monica had, not wanting to leave the girl standing alone off the side of a major highway, offered to take Elizabeth the final few miles to her father's house.

Elizabeth graciously declined the offer, and after another long moment of trying to convince her otherwise, Monica decided to give in to Elizabeth's wishes. She merged back onto the highway alone, leaving Elizabeth sitting down on the walkway, throwing rocks across the empty parking lot.

As Monica continued to drive, an overwhelming feeling of fatigue began to consume her. After stopping at a gas station to fill her tank, which she came to realize was not as efficient as she had originally thought, and waiting at a stop sign for it to turn green, she decided it was in her best interest to find a place to spend the night.

She debated momentarily whether or not she should sleep in the van again (she felt less secure without Isaiah's presence) or rent a motel room for the night.

With her wallet always sitting at the forefront of her mind, she decided to once again find an empty parking lot to pass a few unconscious hours.

What If We Woke Up?

She woke up to the sunrise the next morning and watched it over her shoulder as she began driving south again.

Rolling to a stop at a red light before merging onto the highway, Monica's eye was caught by a shaggy looking man holding a piece of cardboard. As the man slowly walked through the row of resting cars, she got a better look at the sign, which, coincidently, stated that this man was looking for a ride south.

Monica looked at the drivers around her, who were all desperately trying to avoid making eye contact with the man. Some rolled up their windows or turned on their radios.

Monica had never understood some people's aversion to offering a helping hand. A few years before her road trip, Monica had befriended a man that lived on a trail close to her house. Because Monica had oftentimes spent her afternoons walking along this trail by herself, she had on many occasions nodded to this man in passing. After seeing him a few times, she decided to stop and talk to him.

One day, after Monica saw a woman walk by the man and look the other way, she decided to conduct an experiment of sorts to see how other walkers, joggers, and bikers treated him. She shadowed him as he made his way down the trail and not a single person looked him in the eye. However, when these exercisers approached Monica, who had a fresh haircut and clean clothes, every single one of them smiled, nodded, or at the very least looked at her.

With this in mind, Monica took another look at the man at the intersection and stuck her head out the window. If she didn't offer this man her services, she feared no one else would, everyone thinking it was someone else's problem to fix.

When she offered him the seat beside her, he seemed almost unwilling to believe that someone would have even given him a second glance. When she confirmed she was not joking, his eyes began watering.

After a few minutes of chatting and sharing surface-level, shallow stories about the not-so-personal parts of their lives, Monica asked Daniel where he was intending to go.

"I don't know, man," he said. "I just gotta get outta here."

"All right then," responded Monica. "You just tell me when."

"I ask you something?" Daniel asked with a flick of his head.

"Sure."

"Why'd you stop?"

"Well, technically, I already was stopped and so was every other car-"

"Why'd you say yes?"

"Why not?" Monica turned to look at Daniel, who could not come to terms with the fact that anyone had been so kind, though Monica really hadn't done much.

"If you're tryna get anything outta me, I don't got nothing."

"No, not at all. I've driven a couple of other people, and their reviews were decent."

"They fill out a survey or something?"

"I should've had them do that; I'm sorry."

"That'd make me feel better," Daniel added.

"Don't worry," Monica said with a laugh. "You're fine. Am I fine?"

"What? Yeah."

"Good." They continued down the highway for a moment, Monica focusing on the road ahead of them and Daniel looking out the window, watching the sun rise higher in the sky.

Monica had become increasingly surprised by the sheer number of billboards lining the highway. It seemed to her as she got farther south, the billboards multiplied. She found herself getting distracted trying to read every one of them as they whizzed by, sometimes in her vision only long enough to catch the first few words.

There were advertisements for restaurants, lawyers, clubs, lawyers, churches, lawyers, politicians, hotels, and lawyers. The signs that confused Monica the most, however, were the ones that she could only categorize as threatening religious propaganda.

"Do you have any plans?" Monica asked Daniel, who responded with a desperate expression.

"What?"

"Once you get wherever you're going?"

"I wish I knew," Daniel answered. Monica nodded her head.

"Me too. It's hard, you know. There are so many options."

"But none of them are good."

135

"Seriously."

"I had an okay job."

"What'd you do?" Monica asked.

"Warehouse. Packing. Shipping. Whatever they told me. I was making minimum wage. Either way, I woulda been screwed; my mom was sick, and I was tryna help. I didn't have the money to keep her alive and stay in my house. Neither are good options."

"I'm sorry. I know that doesn't help, but."

"Then there was some word that got around that they were gonna lay some people off. I got a little mad. They fired me then, but then woulda laid me off later anyway. Now we're here. I'm lookin' for someplace else, but no one wants me. My mom died last week, so now I'm just lookin' somewhere new. A fresh start. I gotta find a shower for the interviews. They won't take me if I don't. They'll think it's a risk; I'm dangerous. They don't wanna hear my sad story."

"I'm sure-"

"You wanna know what the worst part is?"

"Please," Monica said.

"The fact that the big wigs are just gettin' richer every single day, and they were gonna lay me off? They sit in their fancy offices in their fancy high rises and drive fancy cars, and I'm not even given a water break. If I take ten seconds to take a sip, I'm gettin' fired. They go on month-long vacations and laugh at us. We're the ones doing their work. I can't afford to get my dying mother a doctor. They're laying me off? Give me a break. It's disgusting."

"I completely agree. They get richer just lounging around. I mean, good for them, I'm sure their fathers would be proud, but the fact that they're just sitting on that money...that's the sickest part. They must run out of things to buy. How many cars do you need? How many boats, how many private jets, how many mansions? I don't get it. They have all the power in the world to make a difference, and yet they're so selfish that they never really help. Yeah, they donate some money. However, I'm sure they're only doing that because of the pressure to do something with it other than indulge themselves. If they were doing it out of the goodness of their hearts, they would be eager to do as much as they could. I read somewhere that some of the donations they've made are the equivalent of the average American donating a dollar or two. They wouldn't even notice if they were missing a lot of money, so why don't they put that to good use? I just don't understand the level of absolute selfishness and ignorance they need to have to engage in that pompous and pretentious way of thinking."

"I'm always confused why they don't pay real taxes."

"Oh, god, don't even get me started. Why? What? I saw some celebrity had made some video a couple of years ago complaining about how much money they lost to taxes. They kept saying they were losing millions, but they were making millions more. No one needs that type of money to live. If they took a little bit more, those rich people could still live in total comfort. At the end of the day, if they own six cars instead of seven, I don't feel bad. So what if they lost a couple more bucks, they'd still be millionaires. I understand it's probably fun to purchase expensive things, but we're twenty-six trillion dollars in debt as a country, people can't afford to eat-"

"Medical care."

"Exactly. They're the ones with the money to make change happen, but they choose to peacock egotistically. The gap between the uber-rich and everyone else only continues to widen because of that."

"The American dream is dead."

"By the time my grandkids are alive, there won't even be a middle class. It'll only be the exploited and the exploiters. It doesn't matter how you do it; you can take from the top or add to the bottom, but either way, something has to be done."

"Exactly."

"When they first get some money, it must be exciting. Eventually, though, I think they kind of have to realize they have a platform they could use. It doesn't matter what issue they choose to lend their bank account to as long as it's getting something done. I don't think I even have to agree with them, if they're doing something to help out, I have to respect that. If they have the ability to make a difference, why don't they?"

"Couldn't tell ya."

"My mother's been paying a large portion of her salary for years just for a place to live. Every dollar that she didn't spend on food or other necessities went to my college fund. There's enough money in that for a semester and a half, and she's been doing that since before I was born. My generation can't afford to educate themselves, but it's necessary if you want a shot at whatever our grandparents considered the American dream. It's so expensive that some people don't even get a chance."

"I don't get it," Daniel said. "Why is it so hard?"

"I'm not by any means saying I know how to fix this kind of stuff, but there are plenty of people that do. Why, instead of wasting money on material things, do the rich not look for these people? They should all be willing to help."

"I'm not one of those people that would wanna live in the woods and not have nothing, you know. I'd like a pretty car. I'd like that kind of stuff, but I think I'd feel guilty if I knew people down the block were starving to death, and I wasn't doin' nothing."

"I honestly think it's repulsive to die with that much money. Even when they do eventually die themselves, that money's going to stay in the family, and those kids are even less likely to be understanding because they've never known what it's really like. Although, their parents never knew either. All of the uber-rich started with a lot of money; some of them even took hundreds of thousands of dollars worth of loans from their parents. Any time someone says they're a self-made billionaire, I take it with a grain (or two) of salt" Monica said.

"Yeah."

"You want to know what else makes me mad?"

"Love to. It probably makes me mad too."

"It should make everyone mad, I think."

"Let's hear it," Daniel suggested.

"Whatever these rich people do, nothing is going to happen to them. Because of the ridiculous amount of privilege they have, they could probably murder someone without that many repercussions, especially if they're white. I just don't understand how that makes any sense. The legal system favors pale rich people. You're treated well if you're white and rich, even if you're guilty. You know how many people can't afford to bail themselves out before they even get a trial? They're sitting there in jail before they're even convicted, or they're forced to plead guilty so they can get on with their lives, and a disproportionate number of them are people of color. These rich people could bail themselves out a thousand times over and not notice their pockets were any lighter. I don't get super easily frustrated, I really try to stay calm and level headed, but when one day I turned on the news and a woman who could have gotten...I read some reports that said forty years ended up with two months, I kind of lost it. Two months. Two months. Granted, the problem she got herself into was something only a rich white person would do in the first place, but still, that's appalling. Then there's the homeless woman that used someone else's address to register her kid for a better school that gets five years. Five years. Just think about that. Obviously, there were some other moving pieces including the fact that she's black, which is also treated as a crime in America. That just astonishes me. I'm not saying the rich lady should have gotten five years herself, I'm just saying the woman trying to ensure her child gets a good education shouldn't have to suffer through that. Now, I'm not a supporter of the legal system as it is to begin with, but it just gets me fired up. The fact that if you have the money, you can walk around and do whatever you want cause you can afford the best lawyers is inexcusable and is a horrible reflection on the justice system as a whole. They think they're above the law, and in my opinion, that is one of the most corrupt, narcissistic, and greedy facts I have ever heard in my life. If these people focused a little bit less on themselves and their bank statements, they wouldn't get involved in that kind of stuff, *and* they'd be able to help out so many more people."

"It'd probably make them feel good to help out too, you know."

"Exactly. Maybe they'd find a bit more of a purpose in their lives."

"I always think why do we need billionaires in the first place?" Daniel said. We don't. Nobody needs that much. Say I got a good job. I got enough to eat and rent. I lose a lotta money in taxes, though, right? If the richest billionaires lost the same percentage to taxes, they could still comfortably vacation six months outta the year. If they were taxed more, imagine how much better off we all would be. They're so selfish they don't know what just a little bit of their money could do. It's their job to use the money they make from the even bigger companies to help the people that work for those companies."

"Exactly. The rich people should see themselves as a middle-man. It's disgusting they have to understand how much others are struggling, but they choose to think only of themselves. They have so much money, that they're basically able to control a large percentage of the government. If they wanted a candidate to be elected, the billionaires could spend millions and millions on the campaign without really having to do any fundraising. Then, when those people do get elected into office, the billionaires can pretty much control everything the politician stands for. The people aren't elected themselves; they're puppets for the rich people to get whatever they want. Then, they have so much political influence, they can get whatever bills or acts or laws passed, and oftentimes, those bills don't reflect what the country and the majority of its population actually needs. The people at the top of the economic pyramid essentially have full control over everyone else."

"It's not even like they get rich by themselves," Daniel injected.

"They got rich *because* of all the employees they took advantage of. You don't get that rich alone. Morally good people would never allow themselves to reach such a ridiculous level of wealth. Even if they did contribute much to society with their invention or whatever, they have no need for that much money."

"I can't even wrap my head around how much that is. Before I..." Daniel paused. "Well, before I lost my job, I was making minimum wage, right. I just don't understand why I had to, you know, have roommates and cut back on food some nights. If I had any interest in having kids or a pet or anything like that, I woulda ran into some problems. I couldn't afford comfort. My boss sittin' all high and mighty in his office and his swivel chair hired people to raise his kids so he could jet across the country every week. I just don't get why I couldn't afford to eat a second piece of toast or somethin' when he's getting his caviar served on a golden platter. I'm sure you understand why I got so mad when they said I might get laid off, nevermind the fact that I needed the money for my mother on top of it."

"Oh, definitely," Monica said. "I'd be furious."

"I don't think I'm mad at people for earning a decent amount of money; if I got a million, honestly, I'd want to buy a nice house, you know. It's just when they take advantage of other people and then spend the money other people worked hard to earn them on stupid things, that's when I get mad. I'm mad at the system that lets them get that rich. I don't got any ideas for new technology or nothing like that, so I probably won't ever get that much money, and I'm not sayin' I deserve to be rich. I just want to be able to eat when I get hungry and not have to worry about still paying rent. I'm gonna get another job, and I'm probably gonna end up helping some other rich person get even richer in the process. I'd just like it if the bosses treated me more like a human who deserves to live and less like a robot to get them richer."

The Hippie

Monica said her goodbyes to Daniel when she stopped to refuel and get a sandwich. After turning off the highway, the pair searched the nearest town for a gas station. Daniel liked the look of the area so much, he decided it was where he was going to stay.

There were help-wanted signs plastered on storefronts lining the main drag, and Daniel decided he would apply.

Two days after Monica said her final goodbye, Daniel got a job working as a cashier at a chain supermarket. When one man wearing a shirt advertising a local plumbing business went through Daniel's checkout line, Daniel commented on a dream he had had as a teenager to become a plumber himself. This caught the man's interest, and while Daniel rang up a frozen pizza, two six-packs, three sticks of beef jerky, and an apple, the man pulled out his business card.

In time, Daniel himself became a plumber at that man's company. Working for a small, family-owned business, Daniel was treated like a full-fledged person and not another machine. He finally received the respect he had waited so long for.

After saving up for many years, Daniel had enough money to put a down payment on a home of his own.

He developed a passion for landscaping and gardening, and oftentimes, curious walkers and neighbors would stop by to admire his handiwork.

What If We Woke Up?

Daniel kept his mother's ashes on the front windowsill of his home to overlook the traffic and his collection of roses and tulips.

Once Monica's gas tank and stomach were both full, she started down the highway again.

After so many hours driving straight down the east coast, Monica was growing increasingly lonely. For her entire life, in order to fall asleep at night, she would create people, talk to them, and become friends with them, or she would dream of people she already knew. Monica was never lonely because she was able to create realities that existed only in her imagination. She was never really present in the real world because she lived so much in her own fantasies. If Monica had the passion, she would have made a great storyteller.

Monica Lewis had never been away from her mother for more than a single night previously. When she was in elementary school, Monica had been invited to a birthday party that would have necessitated spending the night on the birthday girl's bedroom floor. This girl had not intended to invite Monica in the first place, but when she informed her mom she was going to invite every girl in the class "except for the weird one that doesn't say anything," the mother requested that she not be rude. The girl protested momentarily, but the mother would not stand for such ignorance. When the girl handed Monica her half-hearted invitation, neither was too pleased.

Monica, even at such a young age, understood her presence was not truly welcomed, so she stuffed the poorly folded cardstock into the bottom of her backpack. However, when Katherine was packing Monica's peanut butter and jelly sandwich for the next day, she saw and read the invitation.

Even after Monica pleaded with Katherine to allow her decline, Katherine was insistent that Monica would not grow up to be socially inferior and said her only option was to attend.

Katherine dropped Monica off at six in the afternoon the next weekend and admired the McMansion the birthday girl's family lived in. Although all the houses on the street looked exactly the same and there was not a tree in sight, Katherine aspired to have the means to live in such an affluent neighborhood. The duplex she rented was not nearly as ritzy.

The girl's mother baked a cake and ordered pizzas and tried to supervise the girls to ensure they wouldn't treat Monica the way her daughter had originally.

Although the girls never directly said anything to insult Monica's presence, Monica understood clearly that she was not welcomed as a member of their exclusive group.

This was the only night Monica hadn't slept in her own house during the first eighteen years of her life.

Monica was deep in thought when she noticed a woman standing on the edge of the highway, her thumb pointed upwards. The woman was squinting against the sun and, at the same time, attempting to make direct eye contact with each driver that passed, hoping to guilt them into stopping.

Monica did not feel obligated to stop for this woman but thought her company would offer a distraction from her doubts and fears.

Monica flipped on her turn signal and pressed her brakes, moving onto the shoulder. Before she even came to a full stop, the woman was opening the door and sitting down in the passenger seat.

"Thank god," she said. "I was startin' to think the fuzz'd be the ones to pick me up." Monica looked at the woman, slightly startled. "Start drivin' before you change your mind," the woman added. Monica let out a soft laugh.

"All right then."

'Sierra," the woman said, sticking out her hand.

"What?" Monica asked, glancing down at the woman's open palm. The lines on her hand were caked in dirt.

"Sierra. That's my name."

"Oh," Monica sighed, shaking Sierra's hand.

"Now you tell me what your name is."

"Monica," was the hesitant reply.

"That's groovy."

"People still say groovy?" Monica asked.

"No. I started saying it ironically just to kinda bother my mother, but now I can't stop."

"Oh no."

"Yeah. It's kind of a problem, but it's too late. I can't do anything about it now, so."

"I see."

"Yeah."

"Were you successful at least?" Monica asked.

"At what, dear?"

"Annoying your mom?"

"Oh, honey, yes I was."

"At least you got something out of it."

"Seriously. I told her I wasn't gonna waste my life slaving for the man, and she called me a hippie, so I ran with it."

Monica laughed.

"Yeah," Sierra said. "She wasn't too happy about it, but whatever."

"So what do you wanna do instead?"

"That's the million-dollar question, now isn't it?"

"Sure is," Monica said.

"I don't know, man. What do you wanna do?"

"Well, I had just kinda wanted to do my own thing-"

"Tell me about it."

"Yeah, but now I'm not so sure what that is."

"Can I offer a hand?" Sierra asked.

"Sure," Monica replied, a hint of intrigue in her tone.

"Okay, well right now, I'm just kinda traveling along. Going with the wind. A couple of years ago, I decided I wanted out of the rat race for good, so I met up with some other people who wanted out too, and we decided to just travel the country. We've been just kinda playing some shows; we're not a band or anything like that, but you get the idea. We get some little jobs here and there. Last week some old lady paid me to paint her house; that kind of stuff. It's amazing how self-sufficient you can be if you just reject it all. People say we're crazy, but we're happy. We're peaceful. We're all one family, you know.

"The real world's a total bummer. I don't understand. Everyone's just always so angry at each other. Everyone's always fighting with someone else. They're all just go, go, go all the time, so much so that we wonder if they even live at all. What's the point if you ignore everything, right? We got a little garden, and we just live. We play cards and read poetry and think about life and love and death, all the taboo things people are so afraid of, you know. It's not that we don't understand what's happening in the world, we just don't support it. We hear the news, and it's so upsetting. Reality seems almost like some post-apocalyptic movie. I was so confused before. I was watching the world burn around me, and I was just sitting on the train, heading to work. I was so trapped. I didn't have the money or the platform to do the things I wanted to; I was just another blank face in the crowd of seven billion. There was nothing special about me. There was nothing that was me. Once I died, no one was going to even care to visit my grave or anything after like a generation or two. Like, I have no idea where my great grandparents are buried. I literally don't even know any of their names.

"Everyone wants to make a name for themselves and improve their quality of life, but at the same time, they just keep fighting and arguing over the smallest things, but then they follow along with each other. That's not gonna get anything done. We're not going to make any progress if we keep arguing and not coming to a conclusion. My mother kept pressuring me every time I went back to her house for dinner or whatever to have children and a family. I don't wanna be tied down to that. I don't want to see the world through only my husband or wife and children's eyes. I wanna see the world from all points of view. I don't wanna be shut into the four walls of a house, listening to people bickering over and over and over again about things that don't matter in the long run. I don't wanna love one person. I don't wanna dedicate my life to pleasing someone. I wanna do things because I want to, not because someone tells me I have to."

"I was told I was being dramatic when I said that I didn't want the normal things I've been told so many times are what I should do. I don't want any part in the mundane. There's more to life than money. There's more to life than professional status. There's more to life than follower counts or likes or comments." Monica said.

"Exactly. Exactly," Sierra began. "I've talked to a lot of people, and you know what I've found?"

"What?"

"No one wants to live a normal life. No one wants to conform, but we've made it so scary and disgraceful to step out of the box that everyone's too afraid to do it. Everyone wants to live a fulfilling life, but for a lot of people I've talked to, that's just not possible. I really don't know anyone that wants to sit in an office and become a robot. Everyone wants to be treated with respect and kindness, and I do think that most people want to leave the world a little bit better than they found it, but that's just not the message that's given by the society we live in. We're all just told that for everything to function properly, we should just give in to the monotonous existence that the people before us struggled through. I get there do need to be real people that settle down and conform and get regular jobs, but it doesn't have to be you if you don't want it to be. I never wanted to become one of them, and I think I'm confident enough in my position to stay true to me, even if it does disappoint my family. If I am strong enough to reject it, there's no reason why I should have to live an average life," Sierra said.

"Your family's mad at you for that?"

"Right on. They think I'm wasting my life because I don't want it to be a drag, right? I am the disappointment of my family. Well, me and my uncle are. My grandmother and my mother have the same birthday, so that's always a big get together in my family. So, over Memorial Day weekend, we all got invited to my cousin's house cause he's got a pool and everything. So I got my uncle to come and pick me up (he's like the only one doesn't totally hate my guts). He picked me up on Friday from the campsite I was staying at. I was going to sleep over his house and then go to the party on Saturday. So, we had some fun on Friday night. His girlfriend and a bunch of his buddies were over, and we just kind chatted and drank a little more than a little and played some poker, which by the way, I won two hundred dollars, so whenever you see a sign for a supermarket, that's where you can drop me off cause I wanna get a cake before I go back to the tents."

"Sure," Monica said. "I can drive you the rest of the way; I'm not in any hurry."

"We'll work that out when we get there, how 'bout that?"

"Sounds good to me."

"Groovy. So where was I?"

"You won two hundred dollars."

"Right," Sierra said. "So we show up to the party, me and my uncle at like noon o'clock, and the look my mother gives me...I can't even describe it. It's like she was disgusted by my presence. Now, me and my uncle had already started earlier in the day, so I thought it would be a good idea to just kinda rub it in her face. So I went up to her, and I was like 'Mom, do you have any idea how blitzed I am right now?' and then my uncle came over and we started laughing about it together, and she kicked us out." Sierra began laughing maniacally. "It's great. We are the disappointments of the family, and we're not really too worried about it anymore. They hate us because neither of us has a college degree or nine-to-five. Neither of us is married or has kids. We just aren't like them, and I think that's okay. My uncle was never really good at school; he struggled a lot, and he got made fun of for it. He had a little lisp and had to study a thousand times harder than everyone else just to pass. I wasn't interested in pleasing anyone else, so I didn't have any friends or anything like that, so I was kinda the laughing stock of my school."

"Me too."

"Is that so?"

"Well, no one laughed at me, per se, but they just didn't notice me, you know. I doubt they'd recognize me even if I told them who I was."

"I take it you won't be showin' your face at any reunions," Sierra stated.

"I don't have any plans to, no." Sierra looked off into the distance as Monica focused her attention on the road ahead.

The duo sat in silence for a moment.

"They hate us because we're not like them."

"People hate anything abnormal," Monica asserted.

"Isn't that the way. My uncle has two brothers and a sister, and all of them, according to my mother, are so successful. She's never worked a day in her life, but she married a rich man, my father, and she got a whole lot of money when he divorced her leeching keister. She thinks that makes her better than everyone else, cause she conned her way into a lump sum. Her oldest brother is a neurosurgeon, graduated top of his class, and has a different woman on his arm every weekend. My mom thinks this makes him a successful man. Then there's my uncle, unemployed, barely made it out of high school, no family, everything that my mom thinks is just the end of the world. Their youngest brother just graduated from like one of the best schools in the country with a degree in nursing, which my mom still thinks isn't good enough, but hey, at least it's not me or my uncle."

"That's just..." Monica began, a hint of agitation in her voice. "I don't even know, that's frustrating." Monica never understood the desire to look down on people simply because they had not accumulated a substantial amount of material wealth. Monica thought there was more to life than dollar signs and bank statements.

"Then there's me. Honestly, I think she's madder at me than she is at him because she thinks she raised me to be *better than that*, whatever that means. Anyways, I have two sisters, both younger than me. One of them is studying to become...I think she wants to be an elementary school teacher, and my mom's so proud. The other one, who just had a baby, is nineteen, and she got a lot of heat from my family for that. Like, they basically almost disowned her for it, but they didn't even blame her boyfriend at all. No one said anything to him, and I mean anything, which I kind of took issue with. I didn't think it was the end of the world or anything like they did, but if they treat her like that, shouldn't they treat him the same way, cause it's just as much his fault, no? Fault isn't even the right word. It just seems like a double standard to me. Either way, I tried to support her, you know. I don't think she should have gotten all that; she's gonna be a great mother. That kid's lucky, and I think because of how much she had to go through before he was even born, she's gonna make sure he gets everything he wants. So my mom was furious with her, but once he was born, she was basically like 'no, he's a cute kid, I'll let you back in.' She just wanted to be a grandmother and spoil the kid with candy and toys, so now I'm once again the disappointment."

"Oh god," Monica remarked.

"Yeah," Sierra started. "I think the thing that bothers her most is that her ignorance doesn't really make me mad, you know. I don't care that she doesn't support my life decisions because at the end of the day, we'll all be dead, and her opinion isn't gonna matter anymore."

"Woah."

"Well, that's the reality of it. Sorry to break it to you, but that's the truth. I don't need her approval to be happy. For most of my life, I only wanted her to be proud of me. Everything I did was to please her and make her think I was as worthy as my sisters. I did a couple of beauty pageants for her, even though that wasn't my thing. I'd straighten my hair because my sisters did. I'd pretend to be interested in the guys my sisters swooned over, who were total doofuses anyways. If I'm gonna be honest, my sister's friends were pretty fine themselves, but I'd never tell them that. I'd eat salads for every meal cause 'Sierra, you gotta look good in the pics I'm gonna post.' I'd wear a ton of makeup, and that doesn't bother me or anything, it's just not my thing, you know, but my sisters and mother told me I needed to if I wanted to attract the attention of the airheads (as if that was the only thing I should have cared about). As I got older, I started to care less and less about what they thought, and I started to do things just because I wanted to. I graduated high school, and my mom showed up late because I didn't want to wear the dress she picked out. So I started at the state college, and it was all right, but it just didn't feel right. I knew it wasn't what I was supposed to be doing, but I had no idea what I wanted. I dropped out, and my mom lost it. She started throwing things at me, screaming at me, all that kind of stuff. She threw the tube my sister's baby daddy played video games on at me; that's how mad she was. It probably didn't help that I started laughing, but whatever." Monica chuckled at this herself.

"She stayed mad at me for that for a solid six months," Sierra started. "She didn't even talk to me until she invited me to her stupid little birthday party. She does it just for the attention, and she invites all her other rich friends so she'll get expensive gifts, which she just complains about after. I got a job working the front desk at some office building, and it paid all right. One day I was sitting on the train and thinking about how meaningless my life was, and I just snapped. I called an old friend of a friend who was living out of his van and just basically asked him how I could get in on it. So I met up with his *family*, and that's where I've been ever since. Wait, what was I talking about?"

"What?"

"How did I get here?"

"I don't-"

"Oh, yeah," Sierra said. "So now me and my uncle just show up to those posh parties, drain their coolers, and take off into the woods, and honestly, I've never been happier."

"Good for you," Monica said.

"Why, thank you. Eventually, you'll figure out what you want to do yourself, but honestly, I think you're already on the right track."

"You do?" Monica asked.

"Yeah," Sierra responded. "The fact that you've already taken the steps to carve your own path in this lonely world says a lot about you. You're ready to start living. Most of the people you've known haven't taken those steps themselves, and they'll never be as satisfied as you'll be. Yeah, it's scary. It's terrifying, but you'll be okay. You're stronger than that fear."

"Thank you."

"Sure thing. If you're ever looking for a community of rejectors and nonconformists, come find us, and we'll be happy to welcome you; that's what we stand for. If you want in, you're gonna be treated like the rest of us. How old are you?"

"Eighteen." Sierra paused for a moment.

"I don't think anyone would care. The cops never really come for us anyways. We grow our own grass if you're interested in that. You can have as much or as little body hair as you want. You can love whoever you want. There's no judgment. As long as you're not fighting or arguing or yelling or anything like that, you're more than welcome at any time."

"Thanks for the offer," Monica said, nodding her head.

"We just have one rule."

"Okay."

"No matter what, you do things because you want to, not because other people tell you to. Even if other people are doing it...if you want in...you'll join, not because it's the popular thing to do, but because you want to."

"I like it," Monica said.

"I figured you would. I hate it when people just jump onto whatever bandwagon everyone else is riding. It's honestly surprising how many people do exactly that, even when they say they're doing it only because they want to. If you look deep down into your soul, you'll realize how much of its morals and ideals are based on what everyone else is doing. Before I gave it all up, I spent the last few days of my 'normal' life thinking about how much of my opinions weren't my own. I listened to certain songs because they were popular. I watched certain movies and shows because they were popular and so on. I spoke like everyone else did. I wore the same clothes as everyone else. People always used to argue that students shouldn't have to wear a uniform, but isn't everything the majority of the people already wear pretty much the same?

"I've found this even happens with political and social stuff. Everyone on social media platforms just kind of jumps onto certain trends and hashtags and movements when just five seconds before they were blissfully unaware of any type of injustice at all, which is part of the problem to begin with. Everyone's just so caught up in themselves and their image that they don't take the time to educate themselves on the issues; they just dive right in to prove that they care, to show that they are aware of what's happening, to avoid becoming the outlier who isn't involved. Then it seems almost like a competition to show people how woke they are, but they aren't really. They had no idea what was happening before it was cool. A lot of people only care about issues when it's trendy, and that's part of the problem. Whenever something's in the mainstream media, which is disgustingly biased (sometimes even bordering on propaganda), people decide that they're going to support it too, but once the attention is moved onto other things, they just kind of forget about it and move on with their lives.

Yeah, some people are working tirelessly to make change happen, but at the same time, the majority of people are just chillin' pretending like everything's fine while the world's burning around them."

"I've noticed the same thing myself."

"That's why I think I felt so trapped. I understood what was happening, but I couldn't do anything significant about it by myself, and not many other people were as willing to get into the thick of it."

"Yeah," Monica said.

"Tell me why the earth is becoming uninhabitable, and a lot of people are just ignoring it and going on with their lives like there's nothing wrong? I really don't get it."

"I don't know."

"The world is baking from the inside out, species after species are going extinct, forests are burning, the ocean is rising, and the earth can't sustain this type of population growth. We're running out of natural resources and fossil fuels. Tell me why so much money is spent on preparing for war instead of saving the planet, saving the people. I don't understand."

"I'm afraid I can't offer much assistance either," Monica added.

"You know how little money is allocated to education, which in my opinion, is one of the most important things the government can offer, compared to the money spent on overfilling prisons with good people and making nuclear weapon after nuclear weapon, which, if used, essentially means the end of the world? Law enforcement gets a large percentage of city budgets, but if you take the time to think about it, that's just ridiculous. They're defunding school after school, and health care workers can't get the proper equipment to protect themselves, and at the same time, the police have the funds to buy equipment and weapons that basically militarize them. On top of that, police officers are expected to be social workers, mental health experts, and so much more when they barely get any de-escalation training. I'm not saying that individually they're horrible people, I'm just saying when they put on those uniforms, they are partaking in a system that is, at its core, unjust and inherently racist. People are saying the system's broken, but that's not true at all. It was created to work exactly in the way it is: to suppress certain groups of people (people of color, homeless people, disabled people, mentally ill people, low-income people, addicts, and so many more) to give the group the founders belonged to an unhealthy dosage of privilege and ignorance. At this point, I'm not sure the end of the world is really the end of the world."

"What?" Monica asked.

"It'd be a little bit more peaceful, don't you think?"

"I don't-"

"I don't have a death wish or anything like that (well not since I ran away), but whenever I start to think about the state of the union or the world, I can just feel it start to get harder to breathe. Although, I'm not sure I have any solutions to offer, so I probably shouldn't worry about it."

"That's not true. Yeah, individually you might not be able to accomplish the things you'd like, but when you stand with other people who feel the same way as you do, you can

What If We Woke Up?

succeed. When people gather under a common cause, they can't be ignored. If you're passionate about something, I'm sure that means other people are as well and not just one or two but hundreds, maybe even thousands. Everyone has experienced many of the same things you have. They grew up in and live in the same world you do, so they have to feel passionate about the same things you're invested in. You just gotta make a lot of noise, and that's going to attract a lot of attention. I've never in my life felt the need to have all eyes on me. In fact, I, most of the time, preferred to stay silent when it came to irrelevant topics or arguments that I didn't think were important. At the same time, I think it's necessary to speak out and stand up for what you believe in, even if you are scared of the consequences. Sometimes, the topics that you're bringing into the light are more important than your pride, ego, or fear of judgment. I stayed quiet for so long because I thought my voice wasn't loud enough, and I was scared of stepping on some toes or being confronted. However, when you reach a boiling point and become extremely frustrated with the world you have no choice but to live in, you can no longer hold your tongue. Yeah, being judged is terrifying, but at the end of the day, as you said, we'll all be dead, and there won't be any more grudges. If we do speak up and ignite change or at least a more open conversation, that is going to outlive us and make the world a little bit more understanding and compassionate for the next generations. Yeah, I don't know how I feel on some topics because I have not yet experienced them, or I am not yet educated on them, and that's something I do plan to change. If something's bothering me though, if I feel I can spark a conversation by talking about things I am passionate and knowledgeable about, it is my duty to speak up, no matter what other people say about me later. If there is one person that I can help, if there is one person I can make feel a little bit less alone, I have done my duty as an American citizen. There's no reason why, when combined with other passionate and educated people, you can't make a positive difference, and that's a fact." Sierra stared at Monica for a moment, impressed.

"Yeah," she said. "You're welcome in our family at any time."

What If We Woke Up?

The Bartender

When Monica pointed out a sign advertising a supermarket at the next approaching exit, Sierra requested they stop so she could purchase a cake to share with her 'family' when she returned to their welcoming arms.

Sierra instructed Monica that she should leave if she had to, but Monica was in no rush. Instead, she waited in the front seat of the van for Sierra and her cake to return. Monica, for the first time in two days, began to scroll through her social media feeds.

Monica did not have a large personal following, and of those people that at least pretended to be interested in Monica's posts, she had not spoken to a large majority of them and knew them only through association. There were a few long-lost cousins, who promoted their flat Earth agenda, aunts and uncles, whose accounts were only active to argue with strangers behind the protection of their screens, and kids who had been in her high school classes. Travis still followed Monica, and she still followed him. She couldn't bring herself to tap the unfollow button.

She continued to scroll, looking up for a moment to survey her surroundings. Even in the relative comfort of her van, she couldn't help thinking that someone was going to try to kidnap her, steal her car, or whatever else people in supermarket parking lots did. Monica did have a reasonable amount of faith in people and believed they were inherently good, for the most part, but she couldn't help jumping to the worst conclusions on occasion. She locked the van's doors.

She wondered, looking back at her friend's pictures, what people thought of her from the outside. She generally tried to keep herself from pondering other's judgments for the sake of her health, but sometimes her imagination would run wild. She questioned if other people saw her in the same light she saw them or if they thought she was just another outcast that wasn't worth their precious time.

Pausing only momentarily to look at each photo, occasionally dropping a like if the editing was decent and the walls in the background weren't wavy, Monica wondered if these people even knew she existed.

"It doesn't matter," she would tell herself time and time again. "It doesn't matter what they think of me."

Then an even more unsettling thought crossed her mind. What if this lack of worry about what other people thought made her selfish?

What makes a person selfish, she wondered.

Is it the promotion of their own agenda at all times? Is it the disregard for other people's wishes, ideas, or dreams? Is it the inability to see things from other people's points of view? Was she selfish?

Sure, she had tried for the most part to stay in her lane because she didn't think it was her business to worry about other people's business. Did this make her selfish? No one had ever told her that she was, but was it because they thought she was unapproachable?

Does putting one's own happiness over others make them a selfish person? Was she selfish because her main goal in life was to simply do what she wanted? Momentarily, she questioned whether her reluctance to donate every single dollar she had and every minute of her life made her selfish. Monica had always wanted to aid others, but did the fact that she also wanted happiness for herself cancel that sense of compassion she simultaneously felt?

Every image she looked at promoted the standardization of narcissistic tendencies while concurrently making her feel guilty for not being entirely selfless and generous. While some people promoted positivity and good *vibes* on one platform, they posted videos of themselves tearing down other people on other accounts. She eventually concluded that every image she was swiping past was a facade curated to better fit the platform the message was being posted on.

Maybe she was acting selfishly for leaving everything she had ever known behind, but at that moment, she concluded that everyone posting pictures of themselves in trendy outfits with iced coffees and vape pens in hand felt the exact same inadequacy when the cameras were turned off.

This was when Sierra came into view carrying a square cake, a man at her side.

"This is Jeremy," she said, pointing at him with the corner of the box and a nod of her head.

"Nice to meet you," Monica replied in confusion.

"He's just going to the next exit. I figured you could drive us both," Sierra said, opening the passenger side door and plopping herself in the seat. "As long as that's cool with you."

"Um, sure," Monica said softly.

"Groovy."

"I just don't have an extra seat."

"Jeremy?" Sierra turned to look at the man, who was hesitantly watching from the parking lot. "You can just sit on the floor in the back. Is that cool with you?" Sierra asked of Monica.

"Sure." With Monica's confirmation, Jeremy slid open the back door and sat down on the floor, crossing his lanky legs over each other.

Monica put the car in reverse and backed out of the parking spot, glancing at Jeremy in the mirror. He was a tall man, and his head swiveled side to side slowly, his eyes examining every inch of the van's interior. Monica almost laughed at how comical his appearance was, his long legs awkwardly folded underneath him, perching his body forward at an unnatural angle.

As Monica headed for the highway, Jeremy finally spoke.

"I hope this isn't an inconvenience for you, me bein' here and all."

"Oh, no," Monica said. "You're fine."

"I just figured since you were already headed in that direction it wouldn't be a big fuss," he added with a forced laugh. Monica perceived a noticeable shift in the van's energy; Jermey's nervousness was obvious.

"Yeah, don't worry. I don't mind at all."

"Thank you," he said.

"So where are you going?" Monica asked. Jeremy seemed almost relieved to have a clear, easy topic of conversation to ease the awkward tension. This was something Monica understood herself.

Although at eighteen years of age her opinions were concise and well-founded after years of collecting information, she had not always been so confident.

While Monica was growing up, she often found it difficult to start conversations. However, when a potential partner offered a clear topic of discussion, she was not only grateful but also significantly more willing to communicate in the first place.

"Oh, I just had to pick something up from the store over here. I was gonna walk back, but I got a-talkin' with Sierra here, and she said she knew someone that might be able to offer a hand. It's a long walk: woulda taken me the better part of an hour."

"Well, I'm glad I could help." Monica began thinking of the next topic of conversation. Although Jeremy may have been uncomfortable with conversation, she reckoned he would have been even more uncomfortable with silence.

Monica had always found it odd that conversation was the norm and silence was not an option, even when there really was nothing to say. Monica believed many people did not have faith in the power of silence after so many years of listening to people trying to fill the void with nonsense syllables that fell into the pattern of an accepted language. She was convinced that true friendship was built on the foundation that silence was acceptable. She firmly believed everyone should take a little time to reflect on their beliefs instead of screaming to add their voice to the crowd. The loudest in the room may be the most confident, but they are rarely the most accurate.

"Did you buy anything?" she asked.

"Nah. They didn't have what I was looking for."

"Tell her what you were gonna buy," Sierra added. She appeared almost disinterested in the conversation, never taking her eyes off the passing signs (enough with the billboards; Monica was growing tired of trying to read and drive at the same time).

"No," Jeremy added, a smirk on his face. Based on the tone of his voice, Monica was surprised he wasn't blushing.

"Now you gotta tell me," Monica added, watching Jeremy in the rearview mirror.

"I wanted to buy one of those real long candy bars you see sometimes. Well, just cuz."

"He walked for an hour to buy a yard long candy bar, and honestly, I gotta respect that," Sierra added, looking away from the window and at Monica, who began laughing lightly.

"I like it, I like it. Any kind in particular?" Monica asked.

"Nah, just something chocolate," Jeremy said, still inspecting the back of the van. Sierra shifted her body to look back at him and opened the box, showing the cake off to Jeremy.

"This is chocolate," she added. Jeremy's face lit up, and his back straightened. He reached out and peeled one of the cookies lining the perimeter of the cake out of its frosting bed, a smile on his face.

"Thanks," he said, taking a bite. Sierra nodded and closed the box, turning back around.

"So what's your story?" Sierra asked. Silently, Monica wondered if this had been part of her plan all along: to butter him up to make him comfortable enough to really talk. Whether Sierra understood what she was doing or not, Monica gained a new level of respect for her.

"What's my story?" Jeremy repeated. "What do you mean?"

"Well," Sierra started. "Your name is Jeremy, and you *really* like chocolate bars. Other than that, we don't know you at all. So what do we need to know?" Jeremy laughed softly, his anxiousness seemingly decreasing by the second.

"What do y'all wanna know?"

"What do you do?" Monica pitched in.

"As a job?"

"Yeah."

"I work at a bar."

"That's groovy."

"What's it like?" Monica asked. "I was kinda thinking about doing that myself eventually."

"Really?" Jeremy asked, focusing his attention on the back of Monica's head.

"Yeah. I just always thought it would be really interesting to get to talk to people from all over while getting a paycheck at the same time. I've never really been too interested in having any more money than I need (excess isn't attractive), so I can kind of do whatever I want."

"It's freeing," Sierra added. "Getting to go wherever the wind takes you. That's what'll make you happy at the end of the day."

"You'd really wanna do it?" Jeremy asked.

"I think I do. I started without a plan, but I guess that is what I've wanted to do all along. It'd get me to talk to people. I think I'd like to work in a touristy-type area, that way I do get a few locals that I can ask about their wives and children, but also some people that are traveling. Then you'd hear stories from all around the world without ever actually having to leave the country. A couple of years ago I told my mother this, and she was always one to try to pressure me into doing something *she* thought was acceptable-"

"Ain't that the worst," Jeremy interrupted.

"Yeah."

"That's why everyone's so miserable. They just follow the crowd. If all their friends jumped off a bridge, they'd walk over the edge because they'd be so afraid of being the odd one out. They're like cattle," Sierra added, turning to look out the window.

"My mother was like, 'well, maybe you can do that on the weekends or when you retire, but I can't support you choosing that as a career. It's not a career. It's a job, a pastime, a hobby.' Maybe, mother, I don't want a dead-end career, I want a life."

"Yes!" Sierra added with a single clap and a little cheer. "That's what I'm talkin' bout."

"My mother has a friend that just retired, and she got a job at one of those box stores that sells craft supplies and that kind of stuff because that was always her hobby. Before she was really unhappy, and she was taking a few different antidepressants. I applaud people that have the awareness of their state to get the help they need, don't get me wrong.

Anyway, now she's pretty happy, and my mother kept talking about how she hadn't seen her that positive since before I was born. My mother was talking about how good it is for her that she finally found something she was passionate about, but she always knew she was passionate about painting, knitting, crafting, and such. So my question is: why did she allow herself to become so miserable for so many years when she always knew what she enjoyed?"

"I'll tell you why," Sierra began. "Our entire lives we've basically been told what we should want, and that woman just followed the crowd, listened to the majority, and ended up in pain. She was only lost because she had been told what she wanted to find was socially unacceptable."

"If I had told my mother that's what I was going to do, just skip the *actual* career and go right to the good part, she would have lost her mind, which she did."

"Does she know you wanna be a bartender?" Jeremy piped up.

"I wasn't sure I knew for sure just five minutes ago."

"But now you know?"

"Yeah. Can you offer any advice?" Monica asked of Jeremy.

"I don't know, ma'am. I'd think startin' at a chain restaurant as a waiter might be your best bet. You'd probably end up with a few more benefits, better tips, and fewer flies. When you're in need of some medical attention at some point, which will happen eventually, it'd be nice to have half-decent health care. I'd give you a recommendation, but I work for a friend, you see."

"Okay. That's what I'm going to do. Thank you," Monica said.

"You're welcome," Jeremy finished.

Eventually, Monica, Sierra, and Jeremy reached a rest stop and parted ways, never to see each other again. Monica thanked each of them profusely, and they, in turn, thanked her for the ride down the highway.

Sierra wasn't too far from the section of the wilderness she and her beloved 'family' called home.

Jeremy was also close to his mother's home, which is where he lived, taking care of her, washing her dishes, folding her laundry, and cooking her a warm supper every night.

On his walk, Jeremy passed by a small, family-owned convenient store and decided to drop in to see what they sold. In the store, he found exactly what he had traveled so far for: an extra-large chocolate bar. However, he did not regret his day spent looking for something that was less than two miles away from his mother's home. It made him feel good about himself that he had aided a scared and confused teenage girl in her quest for happiness.

The chocolate bar lasted Jeremy's mother for more than three weeks.

Sierra began heading in the opposite direction of Jeremy to her own home. When she eventually arrived as the sun began to set, her tent-mates, friends, and 'family' members were all delighted not just by the cake she served them but mostly by the return of her sunny demeanor.

Although she and her uncle were the disappointments of their family for the rest of their lives, they were each pleased with their decisions.

Sierra continued to dominate her uncle and his friends at the poker table, cleaning their pockets and leaving them to return to their families empty-handed every weekend.

Monica was left to complete the last few hours of her drive in solitude. She was exhausted both physically and mentally from two long days of travel. This was the closest to jet-lag she would ever get in her life.

She never had as much social contact as what she created and engaged in while sitting in the driver's seat of her deceased neighbor's van, her foot pressed against the gas pedal.

This was not the only new thing she had experienced while on her trip to the next phase of her life. In essence, her faith in humanity had been restored. She came to the conclusion that the ideals and beliefs she held to be true regarding the nature of the human race were entirely wrong.

People really did talk. They talked about more than the weather and the game last night and the answer to the previous night's homework. They talked about more than just themselves. Not everything they said could be categorized as a complaint.

They talked about life, love, and the pursuit of happiness. They talked about their fears, insecurities, and doubts openly, even if they had, for their entire lives, been taught that expressing their emotions was an unmistakable sign of weakness.

There were a lot more people in the world that were interested in philosophy, conformity, and freedom than she had originally thought. There were a lot more people in the world that spoke and thought about the same things Monica herself did than she once believed.

Monica came to realize that she had underestimated people. They could be capable of a level of conversation Monica once thought impossible. No one is just an empty body walking around, looking for complete and total guidance; everyone has their own goals for their lives. Everyone desires to leave their mark on the world and make life a little bit easier for the next generations while also following their intuition, passion, and heart.

Monica Lewis, at that moment, began to understand how unique every individual she had ever crossed paths with truly was, and yet at the same time, they all desired one thing above all else. Not acceptance. Not money, fame, power, or popularity. No, they were all fighting for one thing in common: happiness.

She only hoped she would meet people as open, kind, and honest as the people she met once she left the comfort of her van.

The End

Monica Lewis was killed at the age of twenty-four in front of an overpriced Miami parking garage after walking into a drug-deal.

The local news didn't cover the story. In fact, it was only mentioned once in total in the Boston Irish-funny-papers after a few strongly-worded letters from Monica's grandmother.

Monica died holding a chocolate bar, a plastic water bottle, and a pack of cigarettes. She had twelve dollars and thirteen cents to her name.

Monica Lewis was not a smoker, but the man on the street corner she passed every morning on her way to throw only partly edible food at haughty tourists was. Edward was his name, and he had lost everything after his wife drained his bank account, took off with their children, and left him with nothing but a half-empty bottle of vodka and a handful of tainted memories. He went through the bottle in his first night alone and quickly befriended the clerk at the local liquor store. He was fired from his accounting job after it was discovered he was starting his mornings with a White Russian (or two) in a travel mug. After bouncing around between a couple of odd jobs and developing an affection for heroin, Edward found himself living in an alley between restaurants that attracted tourists from all walks of life.

Lawyers from New York City and doctors from Atlanta and teachers from Philadelphia and actors from Los Angeles and engineers from middle-of-the-woods New Hampshire and firefighters from Las Vegas would take their families to dine at the restaurants Edward lived between while on their vacations. At night, he would eat their leftovers.

The owner of the friendlier of the two restaurants had become acquainted with Edward in their time together and would often leave a slice or two of bread in the alley before retiring to his own meager apartment. Some may find it impossible to believe that this owner would live in such a small space (it was less than five-hundred square feet) considering he worked sixteen-hour days and saved every extra penny he had ever earned. The ironic part was that it was often the rich who tipped the man less than necessary. Some thought they were too good to leave a tip at all.

If the owner of the other restaurant found Edward concealed in the shadows of his dumpster, he would have made a call to the boys in blue, who were never too happy (nor trained) to deal with another unfortunate soul.

Monica knew nothing of Edward's story, only that he had somehow found himself at crowded stoplights holding a cardboard sign. Sometimes, he would include information about his children and (former) wife, hoping someone that drove past in their Bentley or Rolls Royce would know something (anything) about their whereabouts; they never did. Edward only wanted one question answered: why?

In reality, it was simply because he became aggressive when he drank, and after the first half of that bottle of vodka, she decided she didn't want to put her two elementary school-aged children through the same trauma he put her through. They had met in high school, and after the birth of their eldest child, they, more out of convenience than want, stayed together.

What If We Woke Up?

Monica walked by Edward one morning and saw the sign (that day there was no mention of his former life). After someone in a used Toyota offered Edward a half-empty pack of cigarettes, Monica decided that she was going to take a quick detour from her usual commute to work to give a large percentage of everything she had to a man she didn't know was named Edward.

She knew there was a gas station a single block in the wrong direction, and after talking to Edward for a moment, she notified him that she would be "right back."

Monica didn't like chocolate bars.

After purchasing a chocolate bar and a pack of cigarettes for Edward and a bottle of water for herself, Monica headed back in Edward's direction. Along her way was a parking garage that people from all walks of life used.

Some parked their Mercedes for an hour or two while walking through Cartier and Louis Vuitton shops. Some parked their Hondas for the night while passing the time in a friend's apartment. Some sold fentanyl. Some bled to death.

Monica Lewis fell into the last group. She was not the first to die on this strip of road over narcotics, and she was not the last.

Even as she lay dying, a young man in his early twenties, who had been pressured into using, abusing, and later selling by his cousin, who would eventually be shot and killed himself, leaning over her, watching her take her last breaths, realizing that an already bad situation had escalated before his eyes, she did not regret anything.

Nothing.

Nothing at all. In fact, she was completely satisfied with her life. She had not let the world convince her to do something she didn't want to do. Although some nights, bouncing from couch to couch, she found herself regretting her decisions (she had always been told she would have made a great lawyer), she did not, in her final moments, regret anything; the physical pain she felt was negligible. The cool metal inside of her, ripping her up, did not cause a sense of impending doom.

She was content. She had gotten everything she had ever wanted: to stay true to herself.

This is why she was not afraid in her last moments. This is why she welcomed the light with open arms. She knew her family would grieve, and she hoped her body would be moved back up to the city that was truly her home, but she did not hold on longer than she needed to. She was ready.

When she told her high school guidance counselor if you had achieved everything you wanted in life, you would not be afraid of dying, she was right. This was the last thought that would ever cross her mind; "I was right."

Although it may not look like a lot on paper, Monica truly had done what she wanted to. She got to meet people. Albeit, it was more often than not her telling them her name and then asking what they wanted for dinner, but she had gotten to connect with people. Rich people. Famous people. Successful people. People that were feuding with their families. People that had been sentenced for crimes they never committed. People who lost their children to wars in their own neighborhood.

Monica did drive from Massachusetts to Miami, Florida.

But Monica Lewis did not pick up a single hitchhiker.

Monica Lewis did not even see a hitchhiker on her drive.

No, Monica Marie Lewis was not crazy.

Monica Lewis always was and always will be a dreamer.

But this wasn't really about Monica, was it?

About the Author

      Emma Claire Gannon would like to, first and foremost, thank you for taking the time to invest your energy into reading her beloved novel. She appreciates it more than she can express in words and is extremely grateful for each and every reader.

      Secondly, she'd also like to take a moment to encourage you to actively participate in some form of activism. Sign a petition, donate a dollar, converse with family, and whatever else you can think of. Every action is a step in the right direction. The world can only become a better place if its citizens are passionate about its well being and actively pursuing improvement.

      She would also like to request that her female readers avoid using rest stop bathrooms by themselves, sleeping in parking lots by themselves, or offering rides to strangers. It is better to be safe than sorry.

      Finally, she politely requests that you check out more of her work at emmaclairegannon.blogspot.com. She is @theemmagannon on all platforms.

Made in the USA
Middletown, DE
01 October 2020